WAIT

A 3000 REASONS SERIES NOVELLA

JAIME P. BRADLEY

For Pete, my husband, my best friend, my Marine. Every romance I write is a love letter to you.

THE CHRISTMAS IT
ALL STARTED (AGAIN)

GINA

*P*olite smile pasted in place, Gina Smith opened the front door to another round of guests, the jingle of bells chiming good cheer from the wreath as it swung.

"Merry Christmas!" She ushered elderly Mr. and Mrs. LaBree through the door, silently cursing the familial guilt and hospitality training that kept her from sneaking out the back door to Dodge, Oklahoma's lone bar instead of putting on this performance. "It's lovely of you to come."

Hopefully her mature, professional veneer would convince most people to keep memories of her teenage self—and all the insane antics that had made her a town legend—from the forefront of their minds.

"Let me take your coats." Natalie appeared by her shoulder, practically glowing in the social atmosphere. But then, Gina's older sister loved starring in their small-town show.

"That's kind of you, dear." Mrs. LaBree fluffed her gray-blue curls and cast a critical eye over Gina before turning back to Natalie. "And congratulations on your engagement."

"Thank you!" Natalie's natural shimmer kicked up a notch.

Gina barely resisted rolling her eyes as her sister thrust out her left hand. The older woman dutifully admired the Buick-sized diamond that twinkled in the colored lights from the entryway tree.

"Isn't it beautiful? Mama's worried because Adam and I haven't been together long, but I'm planning a nice long engagement so the wedding will be perfect. And we just have to make a few changes to Adam's house before I move in." Nat smiled wider. "He's promised to take good care of me."

Gina's lip curled at the dreamy look on Natalie's face. The idea of willingly depending on a partner nearly gave her hives. Though Nat deserved credit. At least her sister had held out and for the right man—despite intense pressure from their mother.

"And what about you, Virginia? Time to move back home and settle down, isn't it?" Mrs. LaBree's reedy voice belied sharp eyes, pointed critically at Gina's bare left hand. The same stink-eye she'd offered as longtime local librarian when Gina had insisted on borrowing nothing but the back-corner romance novels. "You're not getting any younger, dear."

"As lovely as that would be, no." The customer service smile on her face tightened a fraction, but she quickly squashed the urge to stick her tongue out at the judgmental woman. Twenty-seven wasn't geriatric, but in Dodge the gender roles still leaned toward the 1950s. Barbs from the town peanut gallery were why she'd dreaded this Christmas party. Thank god she would fly back home to Delaware the next day. "I have a great job in Wilmington. I'm the new event planner and coordinator for Davidson Hotel."

"Planning weddings for other people?" Mrs. LaBree harrumphed her opinion on that and set off toward the main room after her husband.

"Well, this is fun." It was a good thing she had thick skin. But it would be nice if it didn't get prodded for strength whenever she visited her hometown.

Flicking smooth blond hair over her shoulder, Natalie pried her eyes away from her ring long enough to glance back at her sister. "It could still happen for you, you know."

"I don't want it to happen." Least of all with a Dodge local like for Nat. Gina was going to be married to her career for the foreseeable future, and that was the way she wanted it. With the new job and another year of tight budgeting, she'd be able to move out of her shared apartment and get her own place, even with her current debts. She'd finally have her independence back.

The hopeful thought had Gina tapping her foot to the peppy rendition of "Sleigh Ride" that piped from the sound system. "Remind me why we aren't watching some girl meet an undercover Christmas prince and save a town from ruin while binging on cookies and wine right now?"

"Because we did that last night." Natalie stepped toward the entryway mirror and checked her already perfect red lipstick. "Besides, it's been years since you've made it home for this."

"Thank god." Gina stood up straighter, gazing at herself in the glass as well, but she'd never compare to her willowy sister. "It's fun for you. You're practically the town princess."

A satisfied smile bloomed on Nat's face. "You used to love a party."

"I still do. When I'm in charge of it and not a piece of the floor show." It was a shame, really. There'd been a time when this event highlighted her year. As a kid, she'd run around the house singing Christmas carols at the top of her lungs, holding out a hat for tips. People used to pay her just to shut up.

Nat snorted. "Remember the girl who made it her mission to kiss every member of the band? The one who wore a dress made of duct tape to the Junior prom? And streaked at homecoming?" She fluffed her hair and stepped away from the mirror. "What happened to that girl?"

She finally got burned by her impulsivity, Gina thought. No, not just burned. Incinerated. "I grew up, Nat." The words snapped out, and she deliberately relaxed her tense fingers and softened her voice. "Now I save my theatrics for planning weddings and getting through visits here."

Unoffended, Natalie pressed her lips together and made a

show of sliding a thoughtful arm around her sister. Suspicion hummed under Gina's skin. "I saw him yesterday, you know, in town. He's on leave from the Marines. And he looks good."

The doorbell rang and Nat tugged gently on the glittering pewter snowflake hanging from Gina's ear, dropping her voice to a conspirator-style whisper, ignoring her sister's dramatic eye roll. "It could be fate, Ginny. Your own little Hallmark movie."

"Not this again." Ever since she'd arrived home, Nat had this idea that Gina was destined for the one man—well, one of the men—she'd rather never see again. One of her epic failures. Not the most epic, or the most recent, but one she'd like to leave in the past just the same. "He's your ex-boyfriend!"

"He was your first love."

"It was just a crush, Nat, and more than a decade ago." She shook off her sister and whisper-shouted as the doorbell rang again, this time accompanied by a pair of forceful knocks. "And if you don't leave it alone, I'm going to hack your social accounts and ruin your algorithms with nothing but wedding disaster videos."

"Fine." Nat huffed, her pout twitching when Gina offered a deliberately goofy smile over her shoulder and opened the door. Turning to the guests on the stoop, the smile slipped.

For a moment, eleven years dropped away, and she was sixteen again, staring into Ben Richardson's cool, steady gaze, heart hammering. Dying of embarrassment.

Winter wind slapped Gina's face, and she blinked the image away, the vestigial remains of her teenage heart wobbling. But she refused to go back there.

Even though, damn it, he did look good.

Ben's parents, Bonnie and Matt, stood hunched against the cold in front of him, along with his brother Brian, who'd been a year behind Gina in school. The family looked at her expectantly. With focus, Gina rearranged her face into a welcoming smile and made the appropriate greetings, stepping back to allow them entry.

"Hello, welcome. Can I-oomph—" Bonnie smothered her in a firm hug, moving quickly to repeat the process with Natalie.

"Merry Christmas! Look at you ladies, all grown up and ruling the world. Your parents must be so proud." A whirlwind of warmth and energy, Bonnie slipped off her coat and hat, prodding her husband to do the same. "Is Rob Hernandez here? He's got a tractor we're interested in."

"I believe so." Gina looked to Natalie for confirmation, but her sister was busy glowing, receiving a kiss on the cheek from Ben. Though innocent, the sight prompted an old seed of envy to sprout queasiness in her belly. She squashed it viciously, promising herself she'd indulge her juvenile self-pity later with a couple of shots.

"Come on, my Bonnie-girl." Matt looped an arm around his wife, ever the unified team. "We need to go talk tractors."

"Hey, Ginny, Nat. Great to see y'all." Brian grinned when Gina took his jacket. "Let me buy you a drink later?" He winked and joined the crowd in the main room, and the tension in her shoulders softened. Brian—the exact opposite of his older brother —had always been an outgoing and shameless flirt. In fact, generous warmth and relaxed camaraderie had been a hallmark of the Richardson family.

She'd wished for years that her own were more like them.

Reminding herself it didn't matter, Gina turned back to where Ben and Nat chatted—or more accurately, where Nat prattled on about her life while Ben fed her ego with his silent, singular focus.

"Merry Christmas, Ben," Gina interjected when her sister took a breath. "Can I take your coat?"

"Don't worry. She's all grown up now," teased Nat. "She probably won't steal it."

Ben flicked a guarded glance her way from under serious brows before dropping his jacket onto the pile in her arms without ceremony. The scent of spicy musk and man wafted to her nose, sending her pulse skittering even as embarrassment flushed her cheeks.

The rest of the sentence—the part her sister hadn't said—*like she did in high school* was another embarrassing pothole in a past riddled with craters. When *it* had been his new *Marines* sweatshirt that she'd stolen from Natalie—only to have her sister find her snuggled in it the next morning. And mercilessly teased her about it ever since.

"No. I restrict my stealing to cars now." Though her smile felt like a plastic mask, she made herself look Ben in the eye, the little dig cutting deeper than her sister could know. "Enjoy the party."

Wedging halfway into the closet to give herself a moment to reset, Gina began wrangling the coats onto hangers, muttering to herself. "Let it all go. You're a different person now." She caught herself just as she pressed her nose to the lining of Ben's coat for another hit of his scent—similar to what she remembered, but different—and gave herself a well-deserved mental slap.

Marching herself back to door duty, Gina found the hall empty except for Ben, who now imitated a broodingly handsome statue. The years had added maturity to his muscular frame and face, increasing his hot factor to a mouthwatering degree. He stared, transfixed by the greenery-decked archway entrance to the main room—complete with mistletoe and creepily dangling elves.

"My mom's holiday decorating style is eclectic at best. I'd like to think it's a nod to vintage style. Honestly, I think she's just drawn to Christmas garish. But it's one of the few things she doesn't defer to my dad about, so I support her."

When his mouth twitched, she told herself curiosity had her creeping closer, the way someone might stare at a car crash. Only this one was more than a decade old and she'd been one of those involved.

"Personally, the Santa cows are my favorite. They're in the front living room. You should take a look."

He sent her a suspicious glance, which she considered warranted given their history, but still mildly irritating.

Crossing his arms over his chest, Ben seemed to take up more than his fair share of space, and Gina's eyes got stuck on the way his shoulders and biceps filled the blue fabric of his dress shirt. She wondered if he was as firm as he looked. Digging her fingernails into her palms to keep from reaching to find out, Gina forced herself to turn back toward the front door. But the bell remained stubbornly silent, and she heard words tumbling out before she could stop herself.

"So, how are you?" She waited a beat. Ben had always been quiet, more reserved than the rest of his family. But he'd never been rude. "Oh, I'm fine too. Thanks for asking. Just trying to make it through the holidays."

More silence.

"You know, people use these things called words sometimes?" She'd always had trouble controlling her mouth when he was around, and annoyance peeled away her sense of decorum. "If you string them together in a pattern, and take turns, they build into a conversation. Heard of it? No?"

He huffed out a laugh, and Gina nearly did an end-zone fist pump. "Let's try this again. How are you?"

"Fine."

"And your family? They seem like they're doing well. I always thought they were pretty great, your parents."

"They are. Thanks."

The low scrape of his voice had Gina swallowing hard against the sudden dryness in her throat. "See, was that so hard?" She patted his arm, regretting the move when the contact sent tingling awareness through her fingers.

Their eyes met, held, something passing between them that Gina couldn't quite name. She took a step back, glancing between the increasingly boisterous party guests visible through the great room entry and the persistently silent front door.

"I hoped for some late arrivals. I'm not excited to dive into that." She indicated the crowd.

He frowned, eyeing the jam-packed room like a man preparing for battle.

"Are you afraid to go in there? I mean, I don't totally get why, because everyone's always loved you. And you've got the military hero thing going for you now. But if you are, there's no shame in it." God, she was rambling and couldn't stop. "Me too. A little afraid of that crowd, I mean. Why do you think I'm so committed to door duty? Someone will remind me of the year I set the tablecloth on fire. Jenkin Baker will grab my ass. My parents will try to set me up with some Dodge bachelor desperate enough to have me." She scanned the mass of faces, seeing a flock of gossipy birds ready to peck her to death, and wrapped her arms around herself in unconscious defense. "Everyone looks at me like I'm about to make a scene. Like that thing with you…" She swallowed back the memory. "But I promise. I don't make scenes anymore."

Gina's skin prickled and she glanced at Ben, who stared at her with a furrowed brow, as if she was an abstract painting he couldn't quite figure out. He seemed to be deciding to speak when the doorbell rang. At the same moment, her mother swept into the hall.

"Shoulders back, Virginia. Hunching makes you look sloppy." She pinched Gina's waist lightly. "And go get the door. Your father's expecting a few more people."

Gina straightened, smoothing her hands over her hips with a sigh. Deborah Smith undermined confidence with such skill, she could make a NASA science question gravity.

"My goodness, Benjamin, it's wonderful to see you again. What are you doing over here, and without a drink!" She looped an arm in his. "Thank you for your service. You're our local military hero."

Gina stepped away toward the door, glancing back in time to see the discomfort on Ben's face. "Thank you, ma'am, but I just do my duty."

"You need to tell me all about it." And she practically dragged him into the throng, leaving a cloud of cinnamon and White Diamonds in her wake.

Ben shot her a resigned look over his shoulder, and Gina

wondered if they might have a little more in common than an awkward moment in the past.

Ben

PARTIES and small talk rated about as high on Ben Richardson's list of fun things to do as running mountain climbers in the sand. He accepted them as necessary evils, but he always ended up with grit in his teeth and an ache in his spine.

Everyone in the military eventually got used to the awkwardly probing questions about what they'd done and what they'd seen. It wasn't overly difficult to *yes, ma'am,* and *no, sir* his way through most conversations. And he'd been prepared for the one-two punch of standing in the home of his long-ago ex and her unpredictable sister for the first time in ages. He and Natalie had smoothed things over years ago.

But he hadn't been ready for how much Gina had changed; wouldn't have recognized her if he'd passed her on the street. Gone were the deranged Shirley Temple curls and coke-bottle glasses. But the air of urgency and chaos he remembered so well from her youth still hummed below the surface, albeit strapped down tight beneath a layer of carefully designed sophistication. He'd bet a hundred push-ups the polite smile, the reserved twist style of her pale brass locks, and even the fit of her conservative gray sweater dress—though it did nothing to hide her feminine curves—were all parts of a calculated shield.

With his back to the country Santa cow art collection Gina had mentioned, Ben nursed a beer and surveyed the room. She, evidently, had given up door duty and now circulated the party wearing a big fake smile, refreshing people's drinks, making small talk. Putting on the show of professional hostess.

It was all more interesting than he remembered. Or maybe she was just better at focusing what used to be a kind of theatrical energy into what came out of her sassy mouth.

He felt himself smile when he saw her trying to extricate herself from a conversation with their former high school principal. Her cheeks flushed red, no doubt suffering through some retelling of her youthful antics. There were so many. No wonder she didn't want to be here.

The Gina show amused him but then, he figured it was fair to treat her much the way you would a squirrel in the road. Fun to watch. Cute but unpredictable. Best to slow down and keep at a distance. The hum of awareness in his blood at the sight of her had surprised him, but then, he was only a man.

At least watching her distracted from the knocking vault of apprehension that rattled inside him again as his next deployment approached, just a couple weeks away. He'd deal with that when he got back to San Diego and his unit; in a place he often understood better than his hometown, among his fellow Marines.

"Do we know how to close a deal or what?"

His parents appeared by his side, hands linked, and his father slapped him on the back. "Got that tractor for a steal."

"That's great." Ben clinked his bottle with each of their glasses.

Bonnie's dark eyes crinkled at the edges as she looked up at her husband. "We're a good team."

"Darn right, Bonnie-girl." Matt grinned back at his wife.

A familiar pang squeezed in Ben's chest, knowing how lucky he was to have two parents so perfectly matched and devoted to each other. The ultimate relationship. One he'd been aspiring to— and failing to nail—for years.

Bonnie must have seen something cross his face, because she pressed her cheek to his shoulder, hand still linked to his dad. Ben had hated to admit that his most recent relationship had flopped. Amy hadn't wanted to deal with another deployment. Distance was too stressful and didn't "fulfill her needs" and he got that. It was a lot to ask. Particularly knowing he had a tendency to take things too seriously, too fast.

"Don't rush these things," his mother had said when he'd told her. *"The right person will come around. It takes a particular independence to do well when your partner is constantly going away."* And he knew she was right. But damn, he wanted the security of somebody who got it, got him, so badly he could taste it.

Ben took a sip of his beer, now nearly lukewarm since he'd been nursing it for an hour, but it tasted better than the bitterness in his mouth. He loved his family, but couldn't wait to get out of this party, this town, and away from all the reminders of his shortfalls. At least with his Marines he had a clear-cut job, and he'd never let them down.

"I can't wait to get out of here." Something strange and uncomfortable rolled through his gut when Gina's voice echoed his thoughts. He'd lost himself for a moment, hadn't realized she now stood at his side, watching the partygoers as well.

By now, the temperature of the main room had increased, as had the volume with music, voices, and the flow of spirits. She tipped back the last of a glass of red wine. "You probably don't understand. You have a nice, normal family and status within the community. But then earlier you seemed…"

She trailed off, reconsidered, tipped the glass again to snatch the last drop of alcohol with her tongue. "Your opinion of me couldn't possibly be lower, so I don't have to pretend, or play the role. You won't harass me—I can barely get you to talk. Right?"

Their eyes met for a beat, a surprising connection humming. Ben nodded and she looked away, before continuing.

"'Virginia, why aren't you married? When are you going to move back home and let some nice man take care of you? Aren't you pretty now, without those glasses? Remember when you burned down the tent at Girl Scout camp? When you stole the garden club's Fourth of July parade float? In high school, when you asked Ben Richardson to marry you?' As if I haven't grown up since then. It's like swimming in an ocean and getting caught in a school of damn piranhas." She shook her head. "Oh—and all the deals and handshakes! People should really get these things in writing. They're going to get screwed."

Ben would be the first to admit he didn't always read people well, but it didn't take a rocket scientist to hear the bitterness and hurt in her voice, and he wondered what else had happened in her life to put it there.

"I'm tired of being a sideshow." She gave him a theatrically long look, leaned in, and he got a whiff of something sweet and mildly fruity. "I'm inviting trouble, talking to you like this. The gossips will love it."

Knowing she was right, he angled his body to protect her from the view of the crowded room. "You can't wait to get out of here?" He tapped his bottle against her glass, glanced out the window to where light snow swirled against the window. "Welcome to the club, Snowflake."

She straightened in surprise, pulling her scent with her—a smell he liked better than the canned cinnamon and the heat of all the bodies in the house. Her eyes started smiling before her mouth did. "Wow. You and I having something in common? Who knew?" Gina bit the plumpness of her lower lip and the slight movement caught him, sent a shot of awareness to his gut.

He couldn't quite believe she was the same person. A person who used to express every emotion she felt at top volume the moment she felt it. The sixteen-year-old girl who'd once stood on the band's stage at homecoming holding a mic and proposed to him in front of every man, woman, child, and a few of the cows in Dodge—just moments after he, at nineteen, had his own proposal to her sister, still a senior in high school, declined.

Time and maturity worked wonders, he supposed. Still, he'd always wondered about that girl in that moment. And honestly, what the hell had she been thinking?

"Why'd you do it? You barely even knew me."

Gina fingered the stem of her empty wineglass but didn't pretend to misunderstand. "It's no secret I was impulsive. I had a crush on you. I liked the way you treated Natalie. And in that moment..." She hesitated, touching him with her light green eyes before looking away again. "I saw how alone you were and I just wanted you to know that I saw you, that I cared. And that even if it didn't seem like it, you were important to someone. To me."

An ache burned in his chest and Ben fisted his hands, resisting the urge to reach out and touch her. He'd been riding high from making it through Marine Corps boot camp when he'd proposed, blinded by Natalie's beauty and sweetness. Too sure of how things could be, too young and dumb not to be staggered by her refusal. "Well, thanks, I guess. For caring."

"Aaannd the awkward sharing portion of the show is now over." Taking a half step away that exposed herself to the room, she collected used glasses from a nearby table in a fit of nervous energy. There were things he wanted to ask her, but their private moment seemed to be broken and he couldn't blame her for backing off.

"Things will wind down soon." He raised an eyebrow, calling her lie. Cheeks pink, she gestured with the glasses in her hands, sending a splash of white wine onto the carpet. "I fly back east tomorrow afternoon and I've got to pack."

"Gina, you're flying tomorrow too?" The boom of his father's voice had them both turning. "Ben's on the two o'clock to Denver. How 'bout you? I've been looking at the forecast and there's a big storm coming in."

Ben barely resisted rolling his eyes. Like a lot of farmers, his father was more tuned in to the weather than the local meteorologist.

Matt waved his phone toward them. A big blue blob moved across the screen. "It's going to hit us first, then move north. You'll be lucky if any flights get out."

Bonnie jumped in. "Gina, why don't we drive you and Ben to the airport tomorrow? Let me know your itinerary. There's no sense in having more cars out on the road than necessary, and we've got the big four-wheel drive."

"Oh, I wouldn't want to impose." Gina was a deer in the headlights, voice ratcheting up. "I can get myself—"

He leaned into her ear, gratified when she shivered under his breath. "You promised me no scenes."

She whipped her head around, eyes shooting daggers, but clamped her mouth shut, filling him with absurd joy.

"Not the time to fight, Snowflake," he added. "Take the ride. You'll get out of Dodge and rid of all this history soon enough."

TRUTH OR DARE

GINA

"Hey," Gina poked Ben's shoulder through the crack between the seats in the row ahead of her. "What are you going to watch?"

The drive to the airport had been painless, enjoyable even. His parents dispelled the potential weirdness by singing along to country Christmas music, while Ben's fingers twitched on the door as if he were fighting the urge to throw himself out onto the snowy highway. Which had her chiming in, obviously.

They'd parted ways after security, evading eye contact at the gate. But when her seat was in the row behind his on the plane, she'd given up the pretense of ignoring him.

He let out a long-suffering sigh, as if he'd been waiting for her to nose her way back into his orbit. "John Wick."

"Oh, come on. Everyone loves Keanu, but an action movie? Could you be any more cliché, Marine?" She poked him again, because it felt good and something about him turned her curiosity on full force. "I dare you to watch something with culture. Like *Mamma Mia*."

He rolled his shoulders and grumbled something unintelligible.

"Come on, I dare you. You won't lose your man-card over it."

Ben turned his head and she got a glimpse of his profile. It amused her how well he could frown, as if his entire being could retreat behind the strength of his rusty-brown brows. The movement teased out an affectionate memory, a reminder of the young man she'd once idolized.

"Snowflake." He breathed out the nickname in warning.

"Okay, truth then. We'll start easy. What's your favorite movie?"

"Do you two want to sit together?" The forty-something dark-eyed man seated on Ben's left looked between them. "I don't mind switching."

"Yes, that would be—"

"No, thank you, sir." Ben cut her off.

The man shrugged and turned back to his screen.

"Hey, come on. It could be fun."

He stared at her through the crack, unblinking, and deliberately plugged his earbuds into his ears. Then he turned back in his seat and resolutely ignored her.

"This isn't over." She mumbled to herself, not quite sure why she cared about talking to a rock. Young Gina would have swapped seats with the other passenger, yanked Ben's earbuds out, and forced the issue. Mature, professional Gina let it go, sat back in her seat, and started her movie. If she pouted for the first five minutes, at least he couldn't see.

When they touched down in Denver, Ben sent her one last look before filing off the plane.

"Have a nice life." She gave him a finger wave over the top of the seat.

He only nodded in response, though she thought she caught a hint of a smile.

She gathered her things and took her place in the line to deplane. The odd goodbye left her feeling more melancholy than it should have. She had her own life she had to get back to, a great new job, good friends, a future with independence. That something inside her might cling to a good-looking ghost from her past irritated her.

Imagining herself back to Delaware and getting started helped her smother the lingering feelings with determination. By the time she came out of the airport bathroom and turned on her phone, she felt more in control.

Her phone pinged with the alert from the airline: *743 Philadelphia: Delayed.*

Mumbling a curse, she tightened her grip on her rolling suitcase and headed to her gate, sparing a single longing look at the four-thousand-dollar-a-cup airport coffee she wanted but couldn't afford to splurge on. She'd filled her water bottle and had snacks she'd pilfered from her parents' pantry.

When she arrived at her gate, the space overflowed with other Christmas day travelers. Gina bit back a muffled scream, reminded herself that there were worse places than the Denver airport to be stuck for a few extra hours. But patience had never been her greatest attribute and her anxiety climbed as she passed row after row of filled waiting area seats.

She finally found a spot on the floor next to a pillar by the window, well into the adjacent gate area. And realized that she recognized the muscled body lounged against the window just a couple of feet away.

Gina turned around, spotting the gate display adjacent to hers, *492 San Diego: Delayed.* Pressing a finger to her forehead against the tension mounting there, she wondered why fate had thrown Ben in her face yet again. Did she want to curl up next to him and poke until he smiled? Yes. Did she also hope to never see him again? Yes.

Her phone buzzed in her hand and she looked down.

Unknown: Are you stalking me?

Gina whipped around. Ben glanced up, raised one eyebrow, and then went back to reading a well-used copy of *The Dog Stars.*

Her eyes narrowed.

He thought he was so funny, so damn perfect, with his loving family and normalcy and air of confidence. And those dark forest eyes. His stupid hard body. And the scruff of his five o'clock shadow on his sculpted jaw making him look like a model instead of unkempt. Even the dumb airport lights seemed to admire him, shining down on his head, revealing the auburn tint of his military short hair.

Plus, the way he could studiously sit there and read—the very same book she currently read on her ebook—ignoring her. It was annoying. She frowned, poked at her phone screen.

Gina: You wish.

Gina: Also, how did you get my number?

The war between attraction and irritation simmered low in her belly as she plopped down in the free spot by the pillar. She knew she had to chill out. This could be fun. They were both stuck, both had time to kill. They'd just ignore each other for a while and eventually she'd harass him into conversation. Or a game. Who knew, maybe they could even be friends.

A little smile crept onto her face at the thought, easing some of the tension behind her eyes. After all, this wasn't the young, handsome man who used to bring her sister flowers when he came to pick her up for a date. The one who patiently waited in the foyer, making small talk with her dad, while Natalie changed her outfit three times. The one who gently cradled Natalie's face when he kissed her goodnight, like he wanted to take care of her forever.

If, as a teen, Gina had desperately wanted someone to give her the same kiss, the same level of patience and understanding, that made sense. But she'd grown up. Now had different needs, different expectations and desires. And Ben was now a thirty-year-old man, matured and experienced. He may not even have that kind of sweetness inside him anymore.

Ben didn't move toward his phone, so she settled in. And for a while it was fine. She kept busy. She texted her friend and supervisor, Carrie, to give her a heads-up about the travel snafu since she'd been scheduled to work the next day. Reviewed her calendar for the week. Sketched out some ideas for marketing the Davidson Hotel event spaces. For a time, the distraction worked. But as the minutes turned to hours, and the snow continued to fall heavily beyond the large windows, Gina's dread piled up too.

After a while, she did a lap of the terminal to stretch her legs before returning to her corner. This time, the sprawl of other passengers forced her to set up directly across from him by the window, close enough that their feet brushed when she sat down. Blowing out a cranky sigh, she dug into her bag for snacks and stared out the window over his shoulder. Ben, meanwhile, seemed to have dropped his heart rate to hibernation mode and barely moved a muscle.

"Want some trail mix?" Gina opened the bag. Ate a peanut. "Hungry? Thirsty? Need a personality transplant?"

When Ben didn't respond, she plucked a raisin and threw it, the shriveled fruit striking him square on the nose. "This one-sided conversation thing is fun. Did you lose the power of speech in the military? Were you always this grumpy? It was a lot more alluring in high school."

"I'm not grumpy." Ben released a long-suffering sigh, closed his book, and sat forward, leaning his elbows on his knees. "Did you always talk so much?"

"Yup." Gina leaned forward too. "But think of all the ways there are to shut me up." The impulsive bout of innuendo slipped out, but she didn't regret it. Especially when Ben's carefully controlled expression didn't change, but his ears turned pink. Ha! He wasn't immune to her. Maybe she annoyed him, shocked him. Or maybe something much more interesting.

"Let's play a game. Truth or dare? Excellent. I'll start. Truth. I hate flying. Not the actual act of being in the air, just the whole being herded like cattle thing. Having security look through my bag like I'm some kind of international terrorist. And waiting. I hate waiting." Gina dug around in her bag and fished out several nips of alcohol she'd stolen from her dad's stash, cracked a vodka and threw one back, making a gagging face as the fire burned down her throat. "Your turn."

Ben's lips fought a smile. "Fine. Truth. I hate country music."

"I'd say I'm surprised, but after the way you looked in the truck this morning, I shouldn't be." She hated that she found him so amusing. She hated that she wanted to talk to him so badly, even though getting him to string more than three words together was like trying to open a rusty lawn chair. The addictive thrill of triumph when he finally opened up felt good. And she wanted more. "But still." She shook her head, incredulous. "You are a country boy, a rancher's son. And you hate country music?"

Extracting a nip from the pile, Ben examined the label for a moment. "Passionately." Taking a drink, his face twisted. "Ugh, this stuff is rough."

She drank another mini bottle, the burn of cheap whiskey making her eyes water and her limbs feel loose. "Truth. My mother makes me crazy and I'm glad I live thousands of miles away. Which makes me a terrible daughter." She dumped a handful of trail mix onto the dip of fabric where her skirt made a hammock between her thighs, separated the nuts from the fruit and candy.

"Your mother's love language is micromanagement." Ben stole some peanuts while she gaped at him, and he tossed them into his mouth. He chewed, met her gaze steadily. "Truth. Cattle hate me. The horses and I get on fine, but by the time I was fifteen, after one too many stampedes, I got relegated to tractor and grunt work. No cattle handling."

"Really?" Her eyebrows nearly touched her hairline as she realized she'd misjudged him and all his seeming perfection. His parents loved and valued him, she'd seen that, but the intricacies of the family weren't all they'd seemed.

Gina understood that with family, even minor differences

could make you feel like a square peg in a round hole. Knowing Mr. Perfect Marine didn't fit exactly somehow made her feel better about her own complicated family dynamics.

"Really." A shadow passed over his face. "It's fine. Sucked to be stuck in the shop when there was other work to be done, and made me feel like an idiot. Still does." He frowned at her. "Don't you dare feel bad for me."

"I wouldn't dream of it." A little confused by his revelations, Gina blew out a breath, needing to put them on more equal footing. "Truth. I wore a tie every day to school during ninth grade. You probably don't remember, since you were a senior. Just about sent my mother into premature menopause. She thought I was a lesbian, 'not that there's anything wrong with that' she'd always say. But it freaked her out." Gina rolled her eyes at the memory of her mother's dated judgment and veiled prejudice. "I liked the ties. Made me feel businesslike."

"You seem businesslike now." Ben tipped back the last tiny bottle, face twisting. "At least when you're talking to anyone but me."

"I know, right? I can play the part." A small smile warmed her cheeks along with the alcohol. "You make me forget to reel myself in. It's actually very irritating."

Their gazes locked for a beat and Gina's chest tightened, feeling things she shouldn't be feeling. She shook herself and her foot brushed Ben's thigh, the small touch forcing her to realize how hyperaware of him she'd become. They needed to lighten things up. "All right, dare time."

Ben rolled his shoulders as if she was a burden he couldn't shake. "I dare you to…do a dance."

Gina rolled her eyes. "Easy." She scooped up the candies from her skirt bowl, tossed them in her mouth and stood, swaying her hips and shaking her booty while singing *Dancing Queen*, earning little more than a glance from the preoccupied passengers waiting at the gate. And when Ben hid his laughter behind both arms, she threw in a lawnmower move and the bus driver.

Cackling, she sat back down, closer to him and their knees touched. "It's amazing to me how easily you're embarrassed."

He came out from behind his arms, and the brilliance of his smile sent a shot of warmth through her chest. "It's amazing how immune you are to it."

Gina grinned back, fished a chocolate candy from the trail mix bag. Inching her skirt up on one thigh, she set the candy on top, about halfway to heaven. "I dare you to lick me from here"—heart hammering, she pointed to her knee—"to the chocolate. And then eat it."

His eyebrows edged together. "Look where we are, Snowflake. Are you trying to get us kicked out of the airport?"

"Please. Everyone is staring at their phones. It will take half a second. It's just a game." Her blood thundered in her ears. What the hell was she thinking? So much for outgrowing impulsiveness. "You're not scared, are you?"

"I get to eat the candy?" Ben's voice scraped like gravel, his mouth serious.

She bit her cheek, able to stop a laugh but not the flush that crept up her body. "You get to eat my candy."

His eyes seemed to darken as he looked at the path of her thigh, his shoulders tense. "There are too many people around..."

"Oh, come on! Nothing's exposed." He didn't hesitate about the touch itself, not if the ticking of his jaw was anything to go by. Rather, she sensed his innate reserve held him back from the silly suggestive game. "Big man, the muscly Marine is scared of touching me." Gina sang out the taunt, feeling like a punk kid and loving it.

She tried to keep her face firmly impassive. He hooked a firm hand under her knee, pushed the edge of her skirt up further than she had, and ran his tongue from kneecap to the crease of her hip flexor—capturing the chocolate along the way—while in her head *oh shit* played on repeat.

He sat back quickly, mindful of the gate filled with frustrated travelers, and watched her. "Who's scared now?"

"That was nothing." But her voice wobbled. Gina swallowed, her skin on fire where he touched. "No big deal."

"Your eyes are screaming." Ben shook his head, leaned back against the cool glass. "And we're done with the game."

Ben

THE OVERHEAD MIC crackled with the airline attendant's voice. "Excuse me, folks, I've got some bad news."

Ben had to work hard to rip his eyes from Gina's sassy pink mouth and lower his blood pressure. Earlier, he could tell that his stillness, his quiet, made her nuts. She had all this contained energy, and the longer he went without talking, the more she struggled to keep it all tied up. It amused him. And their little game was amusing too. Letting bits and pieces of himself out to another Dodge misfit felt good.

He hadn't been prepared for how quickly the tone of the game had changed or how much he liked it. The taste of her skin still lingered on his tongue, salty, sweet. It would be easy to binge.

The attendant continued the fairly obvious announcement— the storm grounded all flights until the next morning. Immediately, the gate area was a mass exodus of people, but he continued to lean against the cool glass, more interested in Gina's reaction than anyone else.

She'd whipped out her phone before the end of the announcement and intensely tapped the screen. "Are you going to get a hotel room?"

He shrugged, watching the way her teeth worried her bottom lip as her fingers danced across the screen. "I was going to find a corner of the terminal to sleep." He'd slept in worse places.

"I just got a room in the hotel attached to the airport." Her voice held some of the bravado he remembered from their youth. "One of the last ones they've got. I know it probably makes me sound like a pampered princess, but I refuse to sleep here." Her teeth sank into her lower lip again and a coil of awareness wound in his gut. "I know we annoy each other, but we could share it. Split the cost. Get an actual bed, a quiet place to read your book."

"I don't know." He sat up, back stiff, not sure if he wanted to find out what kind of game Gina might talk him into in a private room. The difference between how she presented herself to the world versus how she acted with him gave him pause. He didn't always read women right, and he'd made mistakes because of it.

But something told him she didn't ask out of the goodness of her heart. For some reason, she needed help. His conscience wouldn't let it be up for discussion. "Seems like a bad idea."

She grinned. "Aren't those the best kind?"

WHAT HAPPENS IN THE AIRPORT...

GINA

*G*ina couldn't stop her mouth as they walked together toward the hotel, weaving through throngs of other stranded passengers, Ben confidently cutting a path for her with his body. She didn't want to explain her relief at splitting the room cost, or the state of her bank account. And anything and everything else seemed to spew out as a result. As if by agreeing to spend more time with her, he'd yanked off the tie-down straps on her self-control.

Thank god her boss wasn't there to see.

"...and that's what really happened to the garden club float. Hardly any damage at all. I weeded the community garden all that summer to make up for it."

A ghost of a smile touched Ben's face, but he didn't comment.

Her need to fill the space between them had her looking at him, hard. From the firmness of his mouth and the powerful line of his jaw to the sure stride of his athletic gait, he had a hard-edged quality that screamed *I've seen things*. "Do you like being a Marine?

"I like the camaraderie. I like that I'm good at it and I know my role."

She could understand that. Gina loved creating a clear event plan and being a part of the execution, without ever being the center of attention herself. Something she used to enjoy but lost the lust for somewhere over the years. She'd like to think it was maturity, but suspected it had more to do with being jaded.

"How much longer are you in? What are you going to do after?" More curious than she ought to be, all things considered, she couldn't stop prodding. "I know nothing about the military."

He shrugged slightly, holding the door open for her. "I just reenlisted. I always figured I'd go back to Dodge afterward, to the ranch. Help out my parents."

"Ew, you couldn't pay me enough to go back to Dodge." She shuddered. "Do you have a specific job in the Marines, besides the ass-kicking part?"

They reached the hotel entrance, and Ben dropped his voice to match the more hushed tones of the lobby compared to the main terminal. "I'm a grunt in the First Battalion. Spend a lot of time in a Humvee."

"Is it dangerous?" She imagined him in uniform. Her knowledge of the Marines was limited to movies and news headlines.

His face went blank. "You don't want to know, Snowflake. Depends on the day. What about you? You work at a hotel or something, right?"

"I'm the event planner and coordinator for Davidson Hotels."

He veered into the hotel bar and restaurant, and Gina couldn't help wondering if he wanted to avoid being alone with her. But since it was past dinnertime and her stomach rumbled, she didn't question it. They sat at the bar, squishing onto the last two available stools. Their arms brushed as they got settled, sending bolts of heat across her skin and right down to her core.

"It's a small chain, family owned." Her voice sounded slightly breathless. "We have four locations, but I work at the downtown Wilmington branch. It's the largest."

"Events like?"

"Weddings, business meetings, baby reveal parties, you name it."

He pinned her with a firm gaze for a beat. "That fits."

Gina squirmed, not sure how she felt about his rapid assessment. "I like it. Eventually, I'd like to move up to the director of events for the entire chain, but I've got to pay my dues first. I only just started this job a few weeks ago. Prior to that, I worked the front desk while I finished college." Years later than she'd ever anticipated, but she'd finally made it.

A tinny instrumental version of "I'll Be Home for Christmas" played over the speakers, and Gina could see herself and Ben reflected, bent and bulbous, in a trio of large red glass ball ornaments in the green garland decorating the back of the bar. The image distracted her, them together, twisted and strange, so that when the bartender smacked down coasters, she jumped.

Ben raised an eyebrow at her, then ordered a beer and a burger. She pretended not to see and asked for sparkling water. Knowing she was already diving into her emergency fund for the cost of the room, Gina ordered a cup of soup. Extra crackers.

Ben eyed her suspiciously. "I can get dinner."

"No, thank you. I pay my own way." Gina made sure her voice was firm. She took care of herself. Needing to have him split the room cost was bad enough. Though, after the game in the airport, maybe it had the potential to be worth their while. If she closed her eyes, she could still feel the delicious fire of his mouth on her thigh. Imagine what they could do if she sweet-talked him into letting loose when they were all alone.

"So, if you love Dodge so much, why are you going back to California so soon?" She meant for the question to come out playfully. "Got a special girl waiting for you under the Christmas tree?"

"Nope." Ben met her eyes and something thick hummed between them. "No girl."

Her throat seemed to close under his gaze, making her words

rasp. "I always figured you'd be married with a couple of kids by now."

He broke the connection, focused on the bottle in his hand. "Me too."

The hint of defeat in his voice hurt, had her listening to her urge to distract him. "We should talk about it."

"We talked about it enough at the party."

His denial reassured her they were on the same wavelength. She reached out, brushing her fingertips over the back of his powerful forearm, lingering there, intending to offer comfort, feeling connection instead.

Gina could see it, as it had been that day, clear blue skies and the whole town along the football field for homecoming. Ben had come home from boot camp and taken Natalie on a walk during halftime, had proposed to her beside the stage where the choral group was about to perform. She'd seen the whole thing. Him getting down on one knee and standing up after Nat had shaken her head in earnest and backed away.

And Gina hadn't been able to stand it, that wounded look on his face. And Nat's pity.

At the time, grabbing the mic and announcing her love for him seemed heroic. Asking him to marry her, while everyone looked on, mouths agape, had seemed like a beautiful moment in her dreamy teenage mind.

Gina looked back on her actions now, and horror still crawled up her spine. "I acted out of youthful idiocy. But why did you do it? Why propose to her? You were both so young."

A sharp breath escaped his lips. "You've met my parents. I wanted that, what they have together—and right out of high school just like they did too. I thought, that's what I'm supposed to do. Find someone to count on, to take care of, to be there for me, help hold down the fort when I'm gone. I thought I had it with Natalie." He held up a hand when Gina opened her mouth. "I've learned over the years that I have a tendency to rush things. To try too hard." His mouth in a firm line, he turned back to her.

"What about you, Gina? Why do you say marriage like it's a four-letter word?"

She sat up straight, noting that it might be the first time he'd called her by her real name, not liking the turn in the conversation. "It's not like I'm anti-marriage. But the few boyfriends I've had made me realize that for now, I'd rather be independent. Not overly committed." Especially after the Dustin disaster, but they weren't getting into that right now. She fingered the edge of the napkin, sourness painting her stomach. "If I let me down, at least I'll see it coming."

Drawing figure eights with his index finger on the circle of condensation from his drink, Ben stared intently at the bar. "Don't have too much in common, do we?"

"Pretty much opposite, I guess." She watched his hand move, wondered why the knowledge depressed her, and had to clear her throat against the melancholy tightness. "So, no hard feelings, right? The past is the past?"

"Deal." He wiped his hand on his napkin and held it out to her. And when their palms met, her body's electric response made her flush.

She swallowed hard, deciding in that moment that their attraction should be an opportunity rather than a dilemma. "Deal."

They ate in companionable silence when their food arrived. After, they went up to the room. Ben took one look at the lone bed and set down his military beige backpack on the floor with a thump.

"How do you want to do this? I can take a pillow, sleep on the floor."

Gina tossed her suitcase onto the bed, doing her best to be casual. She wouldn't let him sleep on the floor. Not if he split the cost. Not if her lady parts had anything to say about it. "We'll share. It's not a big deal."

Jaw working, he turned his back on the offending furniture and started digging through his bag. "I'm going to shower."

"Okay." She sat on the edge of the queen-size bed, watched him shed his shirt and head to the bathroom. Broad shoulders, taut ass. He was really hot if you were into the musclebound silent type. The kind who wanted marriage and tradition. *Not your type.* But even as she told herself that, she covertly reached up to make sure she wasn't drooling.

They definitely needed to have sex tonight.

The trouble was, she genuinely liked Ben. Sure, they had opposite positions on important things. Their hometown. Marriage. But peeling back his layers—difficult as he made it— felt good. She wanted to get them back to the flirty and fun place they'd been while playing truth or dare. A place where she could seduce him without being sleazy.

While he showered, she contemplated her next move. She kicked off her shoes and socks, took out her contacts in exchange for her glasses, and dug around in her own bag for pajamas, thankful she hadn't checked her bag.

She sprawled on the center of the bed in a thin pink sleep shirt when Ben came out of the shower, hips wrapped in a towel. She smiled to herself, watching him without guilt, appreciating the view while he again dug through his bag, purposefully ignoring her.

"So...did you and Nat ever...you know." She knew the answer, Nat had told her years ago. But he didn't know that, and getting a little more closure on that relationship seemed crucial to the next phase of the evening.

"No, not that it's any of your business. And I'm sure you already know, anyway." He paused briefly in his search and Gina's eyes followed the path of a water droplet that traced its way down from the center of his muscled back to the edge of the towel.

"True. No one in Dodge could ever keep their mouth shut. Not for good gossip." She grinned to herself. Now that they had the past cleared up... "And you don't have a girlfriend. And I don't have a boyfriend."

"Established," he grumbled.

"You obviously work out. What do you do, bench press? Run? Climb ropes?"

She enjoyed not feeling like she had to keep herself under wraps with him. He'd already seen nearly the worst of her impulsiveness. He thought little of her, and she didn't care about improving his opinion. If she was lucky, she could even make it a little worse.

"Yes. What the hell you getting at, Snowflake?"

"I'm just saying, objectively, you are very hot."

He froze for a beat, then continued as if he hadn't heard her.

"We should have sex."

Ben turned then. Slow, brows raised, incredulous. And with a light flush streaking his upper chest.

"Oh, come on, don't act surprised." She recrossed her legs, grinned, enjoying his surprise. "We're a couple of single, healthy adults. You licked me earlier."

"That was on a dare. Do you proposition everybody you're snowed in with?"

Gina sat up, crisscross style, liking the idea—and his flustered response—more with every second that passed. "Just the built ones."

He opened his mouth, but nothing came out.

"No pressure. Just some mutual pleasure, an exchange of orgasms." She put her hands up, trying to appear nonthreatening, and did her best not to pant as she took in his powerful chest and washboard abs, lightly dusted with dark hair. The complicated swirl of ink that painted his right pec and shoulder made her lick her lips. "No commitments, no feelings, no talk of marriage or any of that garbage."

"You think commitments and feelings and marriage are garbage? Why am I not surprised?" He had a pair of black athletic shorts bunched in one hand on his hip where the tiny hotel towel had slipped, revealing a chiseled dip that she wanted to follow to its end.

"Not exactly." Gina felt a little flushed herself. "They're fine for some people. But relationships fail no matter how legally binding they are."

"They do. There are no guarantees, just an ideal worth trying to live up to." Ben's jaw ticked; eyes darkly intense in the light of the lone bedside lamp.

"Come on. It's just a little harmless fun." As his stillness dragged, Gina felt the creep of unease, an attraction wound tight against feelings she'd sworn she'd never feel again. She'd let her impulsiveness loose and he was going to throw it in her face. Panic slid out from under the all-too familiar sensation of failure, of rejection. "I mean, I'm sorry. I got the feeling earlier that we had some chemistry, but if you're not interested…"

Gina forced herself to look back into his face, where his hooded gaze burned right through her bravado and set her core on fire.

"Fuck it. Let's do this." And she nearly choked on her tongue as he dropped the towel.

Ben

BEN TOLD himself this wasn't a failure, but an opportunity.

He wasn't so reserved as to think sex had to be relegated to marriage, but close. He'd kept life buttoned up for years, doing his duty, doing the serious dating routine. And he wasn't an impulsive person. Hookups were not how he operated. Ever.

And yet here he was, buck naked and already at half-staff.

His Marine buddies, Ryan and Greer, would have some choice words. Greer's would be, *All right, buddy! Get some!* Ben tried to hear Ryan, the older and saner of the two, but his friend stayed out of it.

Gina's eyes had gone from shocked to feral behind her dark-framed glasses, but she still hadn't moved. Sitting there on the bed, all soft and glowing and sure of herself. She had a sexy librarian thing going on and when she bit her lip, more of his blood rushed south. He fisted his hands against the sudden need to drag her against him.

This was her show. He'd let her run it, but he needed to learn the ground rules. Not because she needed them, but because he did. "I don't do this a lot." Understatement of the century. "Is there anything you don't like or don't do?"

She came to her knees on the bed when he took a step forward, an arm's-length distance still separating them. "No, I tend to be very open-minded." Gina crossed her arms to peel the nightshirt slowly up her body, revealing generous hips covered with a scrap of black lace and full breasts, bare to the world, sending his heart rate into overdrive. "But I'll be clear if don't like something, and also if I do."

A groan shuttered through his chest as he allowed himself to step closer to her outstretched hands. It was insanity, but the thread of attraction had been tightening between them since the party. The chance to stop thinking for a while and just get caught up was too good to resist.

"What about you?" Gina's fingertips grazed his chest, lingering over the tattoo on his shoulder, then skittered down his abs, leaving trails of tingling skin in their wake.

Air stuck in his lungs, but Ben finally found enough to speak as he wrapped his hands around her waist, flexing and kneading down her body, learning her dips and valleys. "I don't want to hit you, or hurt you, or anything too rough. I've had a partner who enjoyed that in the past, but it's not for me. And..."

She pressed a kiss to his chest, locked him in with those seafoam eyes.

"I like missionary the best."

Gina snorted a laugh.

"Are you laughing at me?" He got that he was a traditional guy in a lot of ways. But fuck if he would feel stupid for it. "For wanting to look at you when I make you come?"

"No." Gina looped her arms around him, brought him in the last few inches so that their bodies were millimeters apart. "Especially when you made something so standard much hotter just by saying that."

They stared at each other for a long moment, each beat of silence another shared breath as their mouths drifted closer. Christ, he was completely naked and hadn't even ever kissed her yet. Whenever he figured he had a handle on Gina, she went and kicked the rug right out from under him.

Needing to get them on an even keel, he focused on the warmth of her against his skin, the way her heart raced against his chest. And when he closed the distance between their mouths by tiny degrees, the way his vision pinpointed as the last wisp of air closed under their lips.

When he slid his tongue along hers, she tasted the same as she smelled, like a sun-warmed basket of fruit with just a hint of spice. And when she arched against him, her skin was the softest velvet against his roughness. The sensations muddied his brain, and Ben had to fight the overwhelming urge to throw her back on the mattress and mount her with all the finesse of a bull.

His heart thundered. This kind of sexual interlude was so different from the organic experiences of his past, where each date progressed with predictive intimacy. Without the usual concerns for the future that always weighed on his mind, instinct and desire warred with his need to rein himself in and plan the next move.

Ben tried to focus on just his fingertips, skimming the sides of her breasts, gradually reaching more skin while their mouths tangled, listening to her increasingly distressed whimpers.

"Just touch them," Breathless, Gina pulled back slightly to present her breasts for him to sample. "You don't have to work your way in. I'm a sure thing."

"Don't rush me." He stroked the undersides with his thumbs, testing their weight, while his mouth blazed a trail slowly down from her neck.

"Really, Mr. I-tend-to-rush? Now's when you decide to slow down?"

"Wouldn't kill you to learn some patience."

She made a little sound of frustration, rubbing her hips against his erection in retaliation, setting off a wave of painful tremors so fierce he bit back a curse.

Desperate to maintain a slow pace, Ben turned her, set one knee on the bed behind her so they were both looking in the mirror on the back of the bathroom door that he'd left ajar. She reached back, sliding her hands over his neck and shoulders while he tasted her throat. In the reflection, her pale skin was a contrast against his dark tan from the San Diego sun, and their eyes locked. Seeing them together shocked him at first, but she fit right under his palms and the strangeness quickly turned to molten arousal.

Her delicious warmth pressed against him and he focused on learning her shape and texture, stroking down her body, watching her unravel as he edged closer to her apex with his fingertips, each time veering away at the last moment. It was an addictive thrill, pushing her closer without letting her go. Wrestling with his own control while testing the limits of hers.

Finally, Gina whimpered. "Please, Ben."

"Tell me what you want." If this was their only time together, he wanted it to be right, to give her exactly what she asked, without risk of misunderstanding. His focus narrowed, and she filled it. He refused to let his baggage get in the way. He'd deal with it later.

She twisted, pulling him by the arms, then pushing his shoulders down until he kneeled by the bed. Her eyes were a summer storm, and she stepped wider to make room for his shoulders, presenting her sex without inhibition. "I want your mouth."

"Yes, ma'am." He enjoyed taking his time, seeing how far he could push her, how badly he could make her want. His cock ached and throbbed, but he'd always been patient. And as he slowly licked a path from her knee up her inner thigh, watching her face flood with pleasure, able to enjoy the journey unlike the teasing taste he'd gotten in the airport terminal, he knew it would be worth the pain.

"Don't ma'am me, jarhead." But the command came out on a gasp as Ben dragged his tongue over her clit, circled the bundle of nerves, and stroked again. "And please don't stop."

He feasted, teased and tasted, getting drunk on her flavor, until he sent her over the edge of ecstasy, writhing and calling his name like a curse. And he started all over again.

After the second time, when his muscles shook from the strain of holding his own release in check, Gina dragged him up onto the bed by his head and pushed him onto his back. He tried to steady his breath, the thundering of blood in his veins, as she dove into her suitcase and returned with a condom.

She climbed back on the bed and took his erection down her throat so quickly and fully all the air left his lungs. The room darkened in his eyes so that all he could see was her face. Everything else in his world, his past, the potential danger of the future and the nightmares that came with it fell away. All he could feel was her.

"Careful, Snowflake." His abs shook as she moved, nearly making him lose it. Around his fingers her hair had gone wild, and his hips reflexively thrust. But it was her saucy glance as she drew her mouth slowly up that nearly undid him.

Taking a last lick, Gina sat up and rolled the protection down his length so expertly, Ben knew she must have more sexual experience than he did, and he didn't give a fuck. The room was stuffy with the scent of them, quiet but for their panting breaths and the rustle of the mattress as she straddled him.

He tried to think about baseball. About fighting through the last few miles of a training hump. About being on KP duty, or one of the other hundred lame-ass things he'd had to do in the Marine Corps. Just to make it last a little longer. But as Gina lowered herself down, slowly taking him inside her slick heat, a satisfied, confident smile on her kiss-swollen lips, something happened in his chest, snapping free. She blew him away, rocking deliberately, and a fierceness usually reserved for the battlefield gripped him, had him wrapping himself around her, rolling them so he could claim her under his weight.

Her tightness squeezed while her fingers danced down his spine, wiping every thought from his brain. Ben buried himself in her heat with increasingly erratic thrusts, her moans of encouragement breaking his control until the pressure to explode was too great and he let himself get lost to the pleasure inside her.

Gina

"That was great. I mean it. Top-notch sex."

Ben mumbled a curse and covered his head with a pillow, embarrassment plain.

But Gina wasn't willing to let him escape, a shot of energy and imagination coming with her high. She felt lighter, looser than she had since well before arriving in Dodge, as if under Ben's touch she'd been able to dump all the stress and tension of her family, her past, the holidays, and the flight debacle. She wasn't playing a role with him, or trying to impress. With him, she could be herself.

Ready to grind against him again, she straddled his hips. "No, really, you're good." After a minor struggle, he let her yank the pillow away. "I mean, I am too, but together we're more than good. We're excellent."

His mouth quirked in a small smile. "I won't argue that point."

"Perfect. Then, if you'll allow me, I have a proposition."

"You seem to have a lot of them for me."

She went on as if he hadn't spoken, comfortable with the way his hands had palmed her hips, fingers gently stroking her skin. "I'm going to bend my rule here." She traced the hollow of his collarbone, trying to organize the words that wanted to erupt without thought.

They had enough in common for a certain level of trust, but annoyed each other enough to have chemistry. The risk of deepening feelings was next to zero—particularly with the physical distance that would always stand between them.

Gina bent down, followed the trail of dark ink from his shoulder to the Marines symbol on his right pec with her mouth. His lean body was contained power personified. And appealed to a degree she'd never experienced before.

If, and when, they crossed paths again, she wanted the chance to be with him again.

"Well?"

She sat up, licked her lips. "I'm getting distracted… I think, if you're ever in the greater DC area, or we're both in Dodge…we should get together. Hook-up again."

"I thought you didn't want to talk about the future. Commitments." He flicked a finger under her breast and she shivered in response, her hips automatically rubbing over the part of him that hardened beneath her.

"Not a commitment. An understanding." He'd made her breathless, but she wasn't willing to leave the discussion quite yet. "Good chemistry is hard to find. Having a solid fuck buddy is great, right? Convenient for letting off steam. More intimate than a typical one-night stand, but without all those complicated strings."

"Wouldn't know." His voice was low, face impassive. "Never had one."

"How is that possible?" Surprised, Gina's own voice was in squeak territory. "You're sexy. Single. You have the hot military thing going for you…. I don't get it." She got through life with sex, crying jags, and manic bouts of crafting. Those moments of release were critical to maintaining her day-to-day composure.

His shoulders lifted in the most minute shrug.

"One-night stands though, right? Bar hookups? You've used an app?"

Ben shook his head, watching her with that stone-still face of his.

"You've never Netflix and chilled?" A skitter of unease ran up her spine. "You save sex only for relationships?"

Nod.

"How do you function? How do you manage stress?" She ran her fingers through her hair, not caring that it turned to lumpy, half-curled clumps. The information truly did not compute.

He shrugged again.

"Speak, you overgrown tree trunk. You've been inside me. If you play your cards right, you will be again. I deserve actual words."

He huffed out a laugh. "I've always been seriously dating the women I've slept with. I know that makes me old school. Boring even." He said each word concisely, with just a hint of a smile, but his eyes were guarded, brows intense.

She shouldn't have been surprised. The man practically leaked traditional values from his pores, had such a high regard for his parents' relationship that he'd reached for marriage and kids and the picket fence at the same age most people were sneaking booze and trying to escape their parents' clutches. "That doesn't jive with what I've heard about Marines. I thought you guys were all horndogs."

"Sure. But we differ in commitment to the…execution of those urges." He looked uncomfortable, suddenly taking an intense interest in skimming her belly button with his thumbs. "I'm more comfortable taking it seriously."

Gina's eyes narrowed, confusion leading to suspicion. She leaned forward, palms boxing him in. "Then why would you agree to have sex with me tonight?"

"We're stuck. I like you. You offered. I can be pretty black and white. You're anything but." A hint of a smile curved his lips and she couldn't resist reaching out to feel it, taking a piece of the oddly romantic admission for herself.

"And, honestly, it's selfish. I'm shipping out just after the new year." He paused, pressing a lingering kiss to her fingertips. "Deployments are hard. I have nobody waiting at home for me this time. And a deployment like this one is like, ninety percent boring as hell and ten percent exciting and dangerous. There's always a chance bad stuff happens. So, when a beautiful woman drops this kind of Christmas gift offer in my lap, I ought to take advantage while I'm alive and able. Gives me something to dream about for the next year."

A shiver ran through her and Ben sat up, wrapping his arms around her waist in response to her quake, bringing her closer to his chest. Her world was a protected bubble, difficult and frustrating at times, but ultimately safe. She'd never considered what it must be like for him, for anyone whose life centered in unstable places. What must it feel like to know that any day could be your last? What kind of bravery, what kind of strength would it take to survive that?

"Don't think too much about it." He pressed an open-mouthed kiss to her throat. "Seriously. It's usually incredibly boring. A lot of hurry up and wait."

Gina swallowed against the unease that sat like a stone in her stomach, focused on the feel of his warm skin under her hands, as if by touching the expanse of his back she could leave protection in its wake.

Blinking back tears, she tried to keep it light, distracting herself from the ugly potential scenarios that suddenly played in her head. "You like me? I thought I annoyed you."

Ben rubbed the scruff on his chin across the top of her breasts, scratching slightly, then pressed the heat of his mouth there to sooth the skin. She warmed from the inside out, and a part of her feared that it wasn't just because of his skillful touch.

"Annoying, no. Amusing, yes." Ben rolled them and carefully settled his weight over her. Balanced on elbows bracketing her head, he gently brushed back the hairs that had flopped over her forehead. Gina wrapped her legs around him, keeping his hips close. He searched her face, his expression resigned. "I like you. I couldn't be here like this if I didn't."

"Well." Words got stuck in her throat and she had to shove them out, his honesty touching her more deeply than it should. "I'm glad. I like you too."

Skimming her thumb over the cleft of his chin, Gina got caught in the steady tractor-beam of Ben's gaze. She wanted to give him something. Something to make her more memorable than just a couple of orgasms before deployment. She didn't have much, but she seemed to be good at making him smile.

"You should text me when you're bored over there. Or email. Call. Smoke signals. Whatever. I'm always good for a story, jokes. Singing. Bad dances." Putting on her best dental commercial smile, she added, "I can be very entertaining. It's fun trying to get this"—she poked her fingertips into the corners of his mouth and pushed up—"to do this from time to time."

He held steady for a beat before shaking off her fingers with a laugh.

"And when you're done playing soldier—"

"Marines aren't soldiers. Marines are Marines."

"Whatever. When you're done playing Marine in…where exactly? And how long?"

"Afghanistan. Seven months."

"Right. When you come back, you're going to visit your good friend Snowflake, and I'll give you a homecoming you'll never forget." Gina rolled her hips to emphasize the offer, pleased when he groaned in response. "Deal?"

Ben's mouth quirked and her chest warmed, knowing she'd won. "Deal." And he sealed it with a scorching kiss.

SEVEN MONTHS IN TEXT

BEN

> Snowflake: Howdy Sergeant Tree Trunk. Just wanted to say thanks again for making snow-pocalypse a pleasurable experience. When you string a couple of grunts together, you're fun to talk to. And that thing you do with your tongue? Five stars. Do me a favor and don't get yourself killed, maimed, or otherwise damaged. I mean it.

*B*en smiled at his phone screen; eyes gritty from lack of sleep as he deplaned in San Diego the next evening. He wouldn't complain. The hours with Gina had been the best he'd had in a long time. If he let himself, he might already miss her. But it wasn't like that, so he didn't.

> Ben: Yes.

> Snowflake: You realize that you've made it my personal goal to get you to reply with more than two words.

> Ben: It's on.

> Snowflake: I just got home. Did you find the present I left you?

Ben: The panties?

> Snowflake: Was there some other woman who may have left panties in your bag?

Ben: Six months into deployment, these will be worth big bucks.

> Snowflake: Ha! Ten words.

Ben: Worth it.

> Snowflake: Just remember, I'm not cheap. Get a good price. And take care of yourself.

If he tried to read between the lines, he might've thought she genuinely cared. But she layered in teasing so deftly, he wasn't sure. Though their connection had been surprising and easy, he wouldn't let himself make more of it.

Tucking the phone back in his pocket, Ben stepped through the airport exit, spotting Greer's car just as he pulled up to the arrivals terminal.

"Merry Christmas, man. How's the family?" They exchanged a backslap-hug over the console after he climbed into the passenger seat.

"All good."

Greer, the product of a large, nosy New York family that made Ben's look hands off, glanced at him sideways as he pulled out into exiting traffic. "Anything interesting happen?"

More than he'd expected. Nothing he wanted to gossip about. "Reconnected with a girl I knew in high school."

"Is that Richardson code for you tagged a new future wife?"

Ben released a short laugh, the movement more painful than it should have been. "Not this one. She's the no-strings type, like you."

"Nice." Greer grinned in response, deep dimples winking. "I talked to Ryan just before you landed."

"Yeah?" Their friend had already been at Camp Dwyer for a month.

"He says the winds are easy and the patrols have been quiet."

"Which really means sandstorms and getting lit up." Ben shook his head and looked out the window at the passing palm trees. "That asshole."

"Yeah." Greer blew out a breath. "He also said they had a couple of casualties yesterday. IED. Ryan was there. One was patch and tape. The other was bad."

"Who?" Ben let the fear grip him, recognized it.

"Russ McCarthy. I guess he took it to the leg. They sent him to Germany."

Greer and Ben shared a solemn look. It was part of the deal. "That sucks," Ben finally said. "Russ is a good guy."

"He is." Greer turned the car into the base. "Are you ready for this?"

"As ever, brother." They bumped fists as they went through the checkpoint, and Ben tucked away the image of Gina's kiss-swollen smile, preparing for the dark moments to come.

Ben

February: Month two of seven

AT FIRST, Gina was a pain in the ass. Messaging him a couple times a week, relentlessly prodding, sending a funny meme or innuendo-laden insult, claiming she needed to know he wasn't dead. As annoying and persistent a light at a distance as she'd been in the same room.

Now, several weeks in, she'd become a comforting connection to the real world. He didn't feel any underlying guilt for being away, unlike when he talked to his family. She didn't ask for more and he didn't either. She was just…there. Periodically pushing him out of his shell, as if making him laugh had become her mission.

Snowflake: Update?

Ben: Alive.

Snowflake: More detail or I'm going to call and start singing country.

Ben: I have sand in places that sand is not meant to be.

Snowflake: Ready to come home yet?

Ben: No.

Snowflake: I've figured it out. Marines love to be miserable.

Ben: They call us grunts for a reason.

Snowflake: (Monster eye roll gif) What else do you miss from the states? Is there anything I can send?

Ben: Greer found out about the panties…don't suppose you have a friend who would donate to the cause? I'm not giving these up.

Snowflake: I bet my friend Andrea would do it.

Snowflake: Panties for troops. It's my new nonprofit.

Ben: I'm in favor.

Ben: What do you have going on today?

Snowflake: I've got the day off and the weather's gross. I'm going to watch a movie later. Want a play-by-play? Or we could FaceTime if you're free.

The offer had him sitting heavily on his rack, not sure what to make of it. He looked at his watch, still needing to strip down from duty and get ready for PT before his day ended.

Ben: I could. In a couple hours. If the Wi-Fi stays steady.

Snowflake: It's a date. My idea, my pick. No complaints!

Ben smiled and sat to take off his boots, resisting the automatic urge to read more into it. *It's just a turn of phrase.* But still warmth filled his chest.

"What's got you so happy?" Jack Hodges, his bunkmate, strolled in with Ryan and Mitchell close behind, ready for PT.

"Nothing major. I've got a date to watch a movie with a friend later."

Ryan wedged his giant frame into the lone desk chair. "Just don't do what Mitchell did with his girlfriend last week. They watched *The Notebook.*"

"What's *The Notebook*?" Hodges asked.

"Save me from fucking kids like you." Ryan grabbed the cammie shirt Ben had just stripped off and tossed at Hodges's head. The youngest on their team, it had become obvious that Jack had had an unusually sheltered upbringing—and Ben suspected a rough one as well.

"It's a really sad book." Ben stepped out of his cammie pants and into a pair of athletic shorts, remembering his mother weeping over her morning coffee as she read the last chapters. "And movie."

Mitchell went hands on hips. "I thought it was an old army movie. My girlfriend loves that historical shit."

"How'd that go?" Hodges tossed the shirt back onto Ben's rack.

Mitchell shrugged. "There were tears."

The other men snickered, and Ryan rolled his eyes. "This is with that friend from home, right? The one whose sister you dated." He crossed his arms over his broad chest, sharp eyes assessing Ben closely. "What are you gonna watch?"

"Her movie. Her choice." Ben tied his sneakers and stood up, ignoring that damn squeeze in his chest. "She's running this show."

Gina

April: Month four of seven

"This is dumb." From the screen of her phone, Ben spoke and rubbed a hand over his eyes.

"No, it's not." She didn't bother to take offense, simply propped the device on her office desk and sat in the chair so that he could see her face clearly. "It's something I learned during theater to deal with stage fright. You said you can't sleep. This will help."

"Since when have you ever had stage fright?" His grumpy tone was inexplicably endearing and she bit back a smile.

What had begun with her not-so jokingly requesting some regular proof of life had become a steady friendship. She thought she made life easier for him, offering a touch of normalcy and fun to his time away. Beyond being able to poke a grouchy bear, making him smile, making him talk, making sure he was well, she liked the way he made her feel. Just for caring. Just for being herself, for being there. Needed. Wanted.

He hadn't tired of her relentless poking yet, which surprised her. Unlike men in her past. He kept texting back. A couple of times a month, they watched a movie together. Sometimes his work or the erratic Wi-Fi at the base forced him to cancel, but he always rescheduled. He hadn't gotten sick of her yet.

"I didn't say I did, but it's something I learned. It's a relaxation technique. Done right, it might help you sleep."

"Or you can read me something dry. One of your stock lists. The dialog from the musical of your choice." At her silence, Ben released a long-suffering sigh and lay back against his pillow. "Fine, we'll do it your way first. But I'd be able to sleep fine if the damn heating duct would stop squealing."

"Of course." She kept her voice light, though worry made her stomach tighten. She could hear the high-pitched whine he referred to, but the noise had been in the background for weeks. He never talked about what he did every day or what he saw, but something in the last several days had changed, had strained him. She could see it. "Now close your eyes. Take a deep breath." When he complied, she went on. "I want you to think of a place that's peaceful. A place you've been. The beach, a library, a mountaintop, whatever."

Ben's brow furrowed for a couple of beats. "Got it."

She wished she could reach through the phone and smooth the skin, help him relax. "Where?"

Ben hesitated, let out a long breath. "There's a spot in a pasture back home where the brook runs by a couple of willows." He paused, and she watched him orient himself in the setting, the place. "And when the wind blows, it whistles between the trees. Brian always thought it was creepy, but I like it. In late spring, the grasses move in the wind and it's like looking at a green ocean."

"Good. Take another deep breath, in for three, hold for three, out for three. Now, you're standing there." He was probably homesick for Dodge. Not a feeling she understood. She didn't have that kind of relationship with their hometown, not with the landscape. But she could appreciate the sense of peace it could bring him. "The sun's warm on your face and the air smells sweet and green, like it just rained. The grass is moving in the breeze. If you reach down, it would tickle your fingers."

The phone lowered to his chest and her view went black but she kept talking, slow and soothing. "The wind is whistling through those trees and you can hear the brook. There are a pair of sparrows in the branches of the trees, building a nest. There isn't a cloud in the sky. You take a deep breath…"

Gina let her voice trail off, taking a moment to picture herself there with him. But she didn't fit. And knowing it made her a little sad. She simply didn't belong in a small-town life; not in Dodge, where people were so committed to putting her in a particular box.

The squealing whine of the heating duct continued on the other end of the line, but Ben had gone quiet, the slight rustle of the phone against his shirt the only noise. Gina forced herself to smile. Success.

She needed to get back to work. She had a meeting with a client in half an hour and needed to review her notes, get back to her real life and responsibilities. Though she'd done what she'd set out to do, helped her friend, it was tempting to leave the connection open between them, just a little longer. Just because.

But there was a lot more between her and Ben than distance, she thought, and hit end.

Gina
June: Month six of seven

"DRINKING WINE through a straw feels a little wrong." Gina took another sip of the sweet white, doing her best to talk without moving her lips. "But I'm okay with it."

"We ditch our principles in the name of beauty." Across the kitchen counter, Andrea—who also wore a green detoxifying mask smeared across her face—raised her glass. "Thankfully, I don't have a lot of principles to begin with." She took a long swallow from her straw before tossing a bag of popcorn in the microwave and turning it on.

Gina snorted in response just as Carrie came around the corner, typing furiously on her phone. "Who knew electricians would drink so much? I just got the final bar tally. They outdrank the golf superintendents. I didn't think that was possible." She let out a whoosh of breath, tension obvious in the set of her shoulders, rounding the island and picking up the bottle of Chardonnay. "Do we have a movie picked out yet? Can I get you another glass? I'm going to put together a cheese board."

"Carrie, relax." Gina took the wine from her friend and coworker, noting the shadows under the other woman's eyes. "I'll get more if I need it. Park on the couch and let those girls put your mask on."

"Okay, but let me know if I—"

"Carrie, please. This is a night for celebrating." On the surface, the spa-movie night fun stemmed from the successful conclusion of a four-day electrician's convention the Davidson had hosted—and the signing of a multi-year contract with the convention organizers. Privately, however, they were supporting Carrie and her recent divorce. Just getting Carrie to commit to a night away from work at the hotel was a win. "Take a breath. It is absolutely not the time for you to be waiting on anyone."

Blinking quickly, Carrie nodded. "I know you're right. It's all been a long time coming. Just let me know—"

"I've got her." Andrea hooked an arm around her older sister's neck and dragged her off toward the couch, where Carrie's twin tween daughters were snacking on popcorn. Bowls of snacks and candy, nail polish, and lotions littered the coffee table, and *Chicago* cued up to play.

Gina slid off the island stool to join them when her phone buzzed from the pocket of her sweatpants.

Ben: Finally, back from patrol. What are you
up to?

Seeing his name pop up released a warm flood of relief, as it always did when they wenta more than a few days between texts.

Snowflake: Girls' night. Movies, alcohol, snacks
and beauty.

Ben: What are you going to watch?

Snowflake: Chicago.

Ben: That's another annoying musical, right?
Excuse me while I stab my eyes out. Or maybe
my ears.

"What an ass." But she held back a smile, so that she didn't crack the mask and typed back.

Snowflake: Musicals are not annoying. Stuffy,
uptight people like you are annoying. Mamma
Mia is a joy. Hairspray and Matilda got me
through high school. Don't be a jerk.

Ben: Name calling got no one anywhere. I'm
right, you're wrong. I'm better than you at
everything.

Snowflake: Very mature. What about The
Greatest Showman? You didn't seem to hate that
the other night.

Ben: Hugh Jackman gets a pass. He's Wolverine.

Snowflake: I can't fault your logic. What do you
have going on now?

Ben: Read. Stare at the ceiling for a while.
Work out.

Gina bit her lip, then shrugged and hit the video button. Ben didn't care if she was green. His teasing never had the teeth that truly hurt. She never felt the pressure to impress him or perform that she had with other people. She'd never tell him so, but their friendship had become like a comfortable sweater that she didn't want to take off.

Plus, every time she heard his voice, got to look at his handsome face, she believed he was okay. Safe. That the pocket of worry she carried everywhere she went was for naught. A text was good, but not quite the same.

The screen popped up, and she watched his tired eyes widen. "Hate to break it to you, but something weird is going on with your face."

"This girls' night includes spa treatments. Under all this green, my skin is turning baby smooth. You won't even recognize me, I'll be so beautiful."

"Not possible." A little smile curved his lips and Gina's heart warmed. "Girls' night. Please tell me that includes naked pillow fights." Ben glanced to the side, like there was someone else in the room, but the gray wall behind him didn't give her a clue.

"Sorry, we've got Carrie's twelve-year-old twins here so we'll have to save the naked pillow fights for a different night."

"Bummer. That big business thing at the hotel, that went well? Is that what you're celebrating?"

"Yeah." Her cheeks warmed under the mask, pleased that he would remember things going on in her life when he had so much to worry about for himself. "That and…" She took a few steps back toward the kitchen and lowered her voice. "My friend Carrie's divorce is final. She's finally a free woman."

Ben nodded slowly, mouth flattening, and Gina felt the need to explain. "The marriage has really been over for years, but she works for his family and…it wasn't good. For either of them, honestly. I know I've given you the impression in the past that I'm against marriage. That's not true. But this divorce is a good thing. So, we're celebrating."

"Sure, I know it's complicated." Ben frowned, shrugged, and the chain of his dog tags glinted with the movement. "Breakups are going around. Ryan just got Dear John'd."

"No, I didn't." A deep voice echoed from somewhere across the room. Then a very large, very handsome man with dark blond hair and intense blue eyes joined Ben's face on the screen. "He's making it sound worse than it was. We stopped talking weeks ago. Hi, Gina, I'm Ryan. Nice to meet you."

Ben elbowed him out of the screen. "You mean she finally pulled the trigger on a dead horse?"

"It fizzled out." Ryan called.

Gina choked on a laugh. "Well, it's nice to meet you, Ryan. What are you guys doing there anyway? It must be…" She looked at the clock and did the math in her head. "Four in the morning."

"Training, patrol, PT, sleep like shit. Wash, rinse, repeat." Ben ran a restless hand over his head, disturbing the short locks. "Super boring. Every once in a while, something big happens and we're all on edge for a while. Like today, Hodges almost got himself blown up, wandering into a goddamn minefield to take a piss." He rolled muscular shoulders encased in a Marines T-shirt the color of sand. "It's nice to see a friendly face, though. Especially a pretty green one." Ben stared into the camera, voice even lower than usual, eyes crinkling. "Thanks for giving me a look."

Taking a sip of wine to wet her suddenly dry mouth, Gina stared back, a wash of affection and concern flooding through her. The squeeze in her chest was a warning. He needed to get back to the States, safe, so she could stop worrying, stop caring so much.

Pushing the thought from her mind, Gina took the risk of smiling, despite the cracks it put in her mask.

"Hey, no problem. I—" What was it about him that made her want to give, to share? "I'm glad I got to see you too. Keeps me from drowning in worry." Their eyes held, and she felt his pull, could almost feel his fingers on her cheek if she let herself.

"And look." She swallowed hard, jogged over to the couch,

turning the camera so he could see the other women. "Meet all my green friends."

All the females waved, even Carrie, though cucumbers covered her eyes.

"Hello, boys!" Andrea raised her wine toward the phone. "I'm drinking an extra glass just for you."

Gina watched Ben grin, and Ryan's head pop back into the frame, as well as two other unknown faces, who whistled and laughed along with the view.

"Get the hell out of here." Ben shoved them away with a laugh. "Quit nosing in on my girl—my friend time, I mean."

Gina's heart stumbled at his words, sensing he'd ask for more from her, from their relationship, if he thought she'd give. The physical distance would always keep things simple, the way she needed them to be, even though over the last several months her feelings for him had gone beyond simple. But that was a worry to put away for later, for when he was back stateside.

"You guys are getting a little stir-crazy, I can tell." Hoping to bring more light to his eyes, she turned the camera back on herself and grinned. "Hey, you're almost done, right? Only a month to go. You got this."

"Yeah, about that." Ben dragged a hand through his hair again. "Hodges extended his tour, and Greer and I...we couldn't leave the kid here by himself. I'm team leader and he needs somebody to watch his back, so we..." He looked into the camera, something like apology in his eyes. "We extended too."

A hollow pit opened up in her stomach, nausea rolling in. She cleared her throat, not trusting her voice. "How much longer?"

"Six months."

"Okay. February." She pressed the positive smile back onto her face, though inside she crumbled. He did the right thing for his friend, his teammate. It wasn't about her, or them. She had no claim on him or his time. But she still felt the sting of betrayal. "Well, I'm sure you'll be relieved to know that Nat finally set a date. Apparently, she's finally satisfied with the changes to

Adam's house. Even with your extension, you'll be back in time for the wedding." The words tasted sour in her mouth. "June. You and your family are on the guest list."

"Gee, having to dress up and make small talk. Killer anticipation." But there was more of his natural grump in the tone and, as if he was relieved to be rid of the schedule update, his shoulders relaxed.

"I know, right? Although I love a reason to dress up." The twins squealed with laughter behind her, a welcome distraction. "Hey, I should probably get back to the girls. The green monsters are getting antsy."

"We're good, right?" Ben leaned closer to the camera, eyes searching.

"Of course. I've got my life, you've got yours. You're doing what you need to do. And I'm proud of you." The false brightness began to crack, just like the mask on her face. "Movie date next week, right? It's your turn to pick."

A huff of a laugh escaped his lips, brow furrowed. "Sure."

She held the phone for a moment after he was gone, already missing his face. Hurting more than she had a right to. Hoping he hadn't seen it. He didn't need that on his mind right now.

"Hey, Gina. Are you ready?" Carrie poked her head up from the couch, cucumbers slipping down her cheeks. "Is everything okay?"

"Yeah." She pushed against the needling pain that lanced her chest. It had to be.

JULY EXTENSIONS

BEN

*B*en swore. "You lucky bastard."

Ryan stuffed a couple paperbacks into his seabag, readying for departure back to the States the next day. Ben watched from the doorway, guilt eating him, having just finished a call with his parents. Their regular hired help had been out sick for weeks. The hay swather had conked out again, and the deployment meant Ben missed his semi-annual visit. The one that included servicing and repairing many of the ranches' large equipment because he was better with machinery than anyone else in the family. If he hadn't extended, he might've been able to take some leave, go help out.

"Hey, I did my time. I'm not the one who extended. We all adopted Hodges, but seriously..." Ryan zipped a uniform bag, shaking his head, and Ben knew his friend felt guilty for leaving when the rest of them stayed. "I've got that training in Quantico in a couple of months. You're going to apply, right?" Ryan had been accepted to the Marine Force Fitness Instructor course. The military occupational specialty would take him out of the fleet for several years, potentially right up to his twenty-year mark and retirement.

"I'm thinking about it." Ben had done enough collaborative

instruction during Marine Corps Martial Arts to think he would enjoy the teaching and coaching aspect. He liked PT. The amount of school involved made him pause, but at least exercise science interested him.

"You know, Quantico's not really that far from Wilmington." Ryan looked at him meaningfully.

The deeper root of his guilt made him queasy, and Ben blew out a hard breath, rubbing a hand over his eyes. He'd rather hang out with Gina than go back to Dodge to help his family. She was funny. Smart. Sexy as hell. Just the sound of her voice made his mind quiet. The number of times he'd relived their night together innumerable, trying to feel again the way he had when she'd wrapped herself around him in her sleep.

"Yeah, that crossed my mind." She'd been nothing but supportive of the duty extension. Half the time he couldn't decide if he was glad it hadn't bothered her or hurt that she didn't miss him more. The longer they stayed in touch, the more he wanted to see if what was between them would hold up in person. Assuming she wasn't seeing someone else. He'd never asked, and she'd never told.

Ben leaned against the doorframe, deliberately casual though the thought punched. "I wouldn't mind getting out of the fleet for a while." It would be easier to have a normal life that way. A normal relationship.

"Exactly." Ryan set his backpack on the desk and echoed Ben's thoughts. "I'm looking forward to bankers' hours, man. Time to date, time to figure out what I'm going to do when I get out of the Corps."

"I'll start studying." Ben crossed his arms, the decision settling some of the chaos in his gut. "Get the applications."

"Good." Ryan looked around the empty room. "I can't say I'll miss this place."

"Nothing makes home look better than living in a glorified Conex box." Greer came up behind Ben in the doorway. "Except for maybe living in a hole."

"Been there, done that," Ben and Ryan spoke in unison.

Greer nodded. "Come to think of it, the Conex box is pretty good."

When Ben's pocket buzzed, he pulled out his phone, unable to resist a smile at the sight of Gina's nickname on his screen.

Snowflake: SOS. Which shade of blue do you like better?

Ben looked at the attached photos of two swaths of fabric.

Ben: Is this a trick question? They look the same to me.

Snowflake: For reasons that escape me, my mother and sister have come to Wilmington to do some wedding planning, including choosing fabric for the bridesmaids' dresses and NOTHING is good enough. I've looked at so many shades of blue I think I'm color blind.

Snowflake: And my car is on the fritz again. Work is nuts.

Snowflake: And my mother is my mother.

Snowflake: I'm having A DAY. But you are the last person who I should complain to. Sorry.

Ben: I'd rather hear about your fabric problems than talk to the asshats here any day. What can I do to help?

Snowflake: Thank you. Maybe you can show me your face again soon? Preferably freshly shaved, right out of the shower, no shirt. I'm reliving our glory day (night?) to stay sane.

Snowflake: And seriously, which shade of blue?

Warmth flooded Ben's chest. He often felt like he needed Gina more than she needed him. It felt good to know she thought of him when things were rough. He wanted to do more, wished he could be there to make her day easier.

Ben: Consider it done.

He held the phone out to Ryan and Greer. "Which shade of blue?"

"They both look green to me." Greer tilted his head. "Is it supposed to be green?"

Ryan sighed. "The one on the right. Come on, boys, let's get in another lift before I go so Ben can go hang out with his girl."

Gina

December: Month eleven of thirteen

"Corporal Collins stole the trail mix you sent me." Ben's face was half smashed against a pillow on the screen, ruddy and tan against the white case. She wanted to reach out and touch the dip in his chin, to measure it like she had so many months ago. Gina couldn't remember if it fit only her fingertip or her whole thumb, but it seemed vitally important to know. She knew his voice better now than his body, could barely remember his scent. And it made her feel so damn sad.

"No! What did you do?" She had to yell to be heard over the clamor in the background. It was New Year's Eve and Andrea had dragged her off to a monster party—hosted by she-had-no- idea-who—in a suite at the Westin.

"He gave it to a bunch of orphans. Pissed me off, but you know...they're orphans." He shook his head. "This place...it's so messed up. We helped mess it up. It sucks. You join the military because you want to be one of the good guys, but sometimes I

look around here and wonder what the hell we're doing. It's...
complicated. Frustrating."

"Aww, you softy." Gina's eyes were blurry from alcohol, her
heart hurting for him. Ben's face seemed fuzzy around the edges.
She blinked, wanting the clarity of it. For the past several months
she'd worked hard to be supportive and distracting, fulfilling her
role as a friend even as the strain of worry tried to snap her in
half. "I'll send more. An entire case. Share it with as many
orphans as you can."

Andrea flung an arm around her shoulders, looked down at
Ben. "Hey, hot stuff. When are you bringing your ass back to the
States so I can check you out properly?"

"Oh!" Gina cut Ben off before he could reply. "I forgot to tell
you that I got the apartment! I officially have my own place. No
more roommate for me. I know you'll probably want to go see
your family first, but if you're ever in town..." She waggled her
eyebrows over the screen and Ben laughed, warming her from the
inside out.

"It's only a little bit sketchy." Andrea held her fingers apart an
inch. "Her mom was a royal B about it, but it's not so bad. Only a
few spiders."

"You need help with spiders?" Ben propped himself up on his
elbows. "I can handle spiders."

"Nope. No, thank you. I handle my own spiders. My place, my
spiders." Gina nodded sharply. She'd been waiting too long for a
space of her own to let anyone handle any part of it. Her mother
had been very critical—not surprising—but once Gina got it
painted and everything moved in it would be perfect.

Looking mildly disappointed, Ben nodded. "I'd like that. To
come see your new place and meet your spiders. Maybe I can give
you a hand with something else. I feel like I owe you. You've
been...really important to me this deployment."

Gina swallowed back a swirl of emotions. "It's no problem.
What are friends for?"

She was the one who'd put boundaries on their relationship,

and she stood by them. But she'd yet to tell him she hadn't been involved with anyone else since him, a piece of information she'd barely let herself compute. The honest answer was that she cared. More than she'd ever intended. But that was her problem, not his.

"All right. Well, I should let you get back to the party. Happy New Year, Snowflake. Andrea."

"Wait." She didn't want him to go, feeling too soft and vulnerable not to offer him something. So, she blew him a kiss. "Since you aren't here."

Andrea moved in again. "We're going to kiss a ton of people in a few minutes, but she likes your kisses the best."

Ben's mouth curved, exhaustion and affection in his eyes, and Gina's chest ached.

"That's true." She grinned, trying to send light and joy through the screen so he could feel it. Hanging on to her job as chipper pal like a lifeline. "Happy New Year. Be safe."

Ending the call and stuffing the phone in her purse, Gina took a long, steadying swallow of her champagne.

"You should have told him you needed help with the spiders." Andrea sent a flirty finger wave to a couple of suits standing by the bar. "Guys love to be the protectors, especially a guy like that."

"I don't want him to feel obligated. I think—no, I know—I've been helpful to Ben while he's been away. But he'll be back soon, get back to his regular life in California. Plus, he's got his family. He won't need me." At Andrea's raised eyebrow, Gina shrugged with resignation. "It wouldn't be on purpose, just moving on. The way life goes."

Andrea frowned. "I don't know. If you two do long-distance this well when he's in another country, won't it be easier when he's only a few thousand miles away?"

Gina stared into her glass, watched the bubbles popping like her enthusiasm for the party. "That wasn't the deal."

Andrea's eyes sparkled with mischief. "Well, lady. That's why you change the rules."

Ben
February: Month thirteen, two weeks to go

BEN CHECKED HIS WATCH, levered out of bed and set the battered copy of *The Martian* on his pillow for later.

Like clockwork, Greer stepped into the doorway. "Ready to go?"

"Just a sec." Ben's phone buzzed and he glanced at the message from Gina.

> Snowflake: (Reel of a toddler swearing.) This is my actual current bridezilla.

He grinned, snapped a pic of Hodges passed out like a drunken sloth in his rack, then sent it to her.

> Ben: This is my live-in toddler.

He shook Hodges awake. "Come on, man, time to go."
Hodges grumbled nonsense but came alive.

> Snowflake: Aww he's cute. I'd kill for those eyelashes. Much nicer than the woman I'm dealing with. I think her bridal party is about to revolt.

> Snowflake: Seriously, I might have to have Carrie step in with this one. She's so much more patient.

> Ben: Take a couple deep breaths. You're going to blow that bride and everybody else away. You're amazing.

He hoped she listened. They'd FaceTime called earlier, and

she'd shown him the ballroom for the wedding that the Davidson hosted that night. It was amazing, and he'd told her as much, impressed by all the details that she coordinated. But frequently, it seemed like she didn't quite believe him. Like she had to prove herself, not just to others, but to herself. And she never quite believed.

Snowflake: Thanks. I look forward to this one being over.

Join the club. Ben was glad he'd stayed on with Greer and Hodges, but the nobility of the job had worn off and he looked forward to a break.

"All good?" Greer leaned against the doorjamb.

"Yeah." Ben tossed his phone onto the desk, strapped on his flak vest, and gave himself a once-over to prepare for patrol.

"How's Gina?"

"Fine. About ready to rip the false eyelashes off some bridezilla, apparently."

That got a laugh. "You going to go see her when we get back?" Greer asked as they walked out, Hodges trailing behind, still half awake.

Ben shrugged, the afternoon sun blazing even as icy wind whipped his face. He put on his sunglasses and adjusted his helmet. "We'll see. I should go see my parents. But I'd like to. She's a good friend."

"My Spidey sense tells me you're a big fucking liar. I think you're already in deep." Greer's dark eyes went serious, his own dark romantic history shimmering toward the surface. "Careful, man. Just make sure she's not like Amy."

Ben shook his head. "It's not." That, at least, he knew. He wasn't going to rush this thing with Gina. They had time. Once he was back, they'd figure it out.

Nodding once, Greer held out his fist and Ben and Hodges bumped it with their own. "All right, see you on the other side."

Ben ran through his vehicle checks and climbed into the Humvee passenger seat, Hodges at the wheel, Mitchell in the turret. They were the second vehicle in the platoon, with Greer and his team in the one behind.

Hodges started singing the first line of the Maroon 5's "One More Night" as soon as they cleared the interior gates of the base, squinting through the dust on the windshield, a mottled but bright in the sun.

Ben jumped in with the next line, lifting his voice over the rumble of the engine, gaze sweeping the sandy landscape as they headed toward one of the more remote checkpoints for patrol. Singing was an easy way to kill time.

Sometime over the last couple months, Ben had gotten in the habit of watching the blowing sand and thinking of that snowy night in Denver, looking out over the sand and rocks and imagining twinkling evergreens and the chill of airport A/C. And his first taste of Gina.

Maybe he could get her back there. In Denver. Halfway between them both, more or less. Right now, five minutes of her teasing would feel good enough, a whole weekend of her laugh, her body, sounded like heaven. She could use a short break from work too, he figured. It would be good for both of them.

The truck bounced hard over a rock as the vehicles turned off the main road, jostling Ben and causing him to miss his turn with the lyrics. His gaze connected with Hodges's always slightly eerie gray eyes for a beat before refocusing on the rig ahead of them. A gust of wind blew the plumes of dust across the sandy landscape. The particles swirled and spun in the air across the ground. It was almost beautiful.

Until the ball of fire appeared, the deafening blast swallowing the Humvee whole.

SAFE AND SOUND

BEN

Three weeks later, his palms were sweating. It was well lit, sand and dust free, a pleasant temperature. A completely safe space. But the clammy flush of anxiety persisted.

Ben discreetly brushed his hands over his thighs as he walked into the visitor's waiting area at Walter Reed Medical Center in Bethesda, Maryland. Ryan stood, catching Ben as he headed toward the door.

"How'd it go?" Ryan glanced between Ben and the door to Mitchell's hospital room.

"Fine."

"You had to see him for yourself." He laid a hand on Ben's shoulder, squeezed, understanding flashing across his face. He'd been through a similar experience with their friend Russ. "It's a numbers game. You deploy enough times, like we have, and this kind of shit is going to happen."

"I know." Ben rolled his shoulders as they walked toward the lobby, wishing the tightness that stubbornly lodged there would ease, even for a minute. "He's going to pull through. It's just…I keep seeing it. And maybe if I'd been paying closer attention—"

"Cut that shit out." Ryan stopped and grabbed Ben's shoulder again, this time hard. "You did everything right, and he's going to live because of it. You didn't plant that IED. It's over, it's done. Now you have to let it fade away, right? Work through it and let it go." Ryan put a mocking twang on his native Californian speech. "Come on, Richardson. This ain't our first rough ride."

Ben blew out a breath and nodded, staring out the sliding doors of the lobby to the unseasonably warm early March evening where water glittered under the streetlights. Rain still felt like a novelty to him after thirteen months in a desert.

Ryan squeezed again, then dropped his hand to pull out the car keys. "What do you want to do?"

Ben looked down at his phone, the only connection with Gina. One he'd let get fragile over the last couple weeks as he'd drawn into himself, the texts between them thinning, even as the concern in hers became more obvious. He needed to settle the restlessness inside his chest, see her, figure out where they stood. Where to go next. Movement forward was going to be vital to his sanity. "I need to go see her."

"Go. That's an order." Ryan tossed the keys toward him with a smile, still cocky about his recent promotion to Gunnery Sergeant.

The key fob was cool and heavy in Ben's hand, and he wondered when he would feel at ease inside a vehicle again. "How are you going to get back?"

"I'll figure it out."

They exchanged nods and Ben charged out into the rain toward the car before he second-guessed his decision.

Just under two hours later, he stood in front of the Davidson Hotel. The wet trees flanking the entrance glittered in the early evening light, coated in the misting moisture that chilled his skin. His uniform still felt like armor he needed to survive as he transitioned back from overseas.

The light bandaging crackled quietly when he carefully flexed his wrist, while the scarred flesh underneath burned with the movement. He'd built up this moment in his mind over the last couple of months, using it to stay sane, to the point where he knew reality could never be as good. Now he just needed it over with. The knowledge propelled him through the revolving front door and into the lobby with gritted teeth.

He should have texted, instead of being rude and showing up unannounced. He only figured she'd be here because she'd mentioned working late recently in preparation for an event that weekend.

Automatically removing his cover and tucking it under his arm, he scanned the nearly empty lobby, noting the couple side-by-side on a couch next to a lit gas fireplace, scrolling their phones, and a man at a high-top table by the bar-café, drinking a beer.

Abs flexed against the persistent flutter of nerves there, Ben approached the front desk, where an attractive but frazzled-looking brunette stabbed at a computer.

"Can I—" she glanced up, blinked, recognition dawning. "Ben?"

"Carrie." He reached over the desk to shake her hand. "Nice to meet you, finally. Is Gina…"

A whirlwind of a blond came flying out of an office next to the front desk. "I've got it, Carrie, if we move the—" She looked up and saw him, stopping dead in her tracks, and his name came out on an exhale. "Ben." The mask of shock transformed slowly into a smile.

Just as the fist in his gut loosened with relief, she launched herself, wrapping her arms around his neck. He caught her, pressed his face to her hair, breathing in the scent he'd been dreaming about for more than a year, letting the tease of it drown the memory of hot metal, gasoline, and scorched flesh.

Gina pulled back abruptly, eyes bright, let out a shuddering breath.

"If you'll excuse me for just a minute, Carrie."

"Take your time." Carrie blinked double-time, a wobbly smile on her face as Gina grabbed his hand and dragged him toward the front door.

She didn't break stride until they were around the corner,

where she drove him with two hands against the damp wall of the building. A car door slammed somewhere nearby and Ben bore down against the instinct to jump, dive for cover.

Her happy reaction to seeing him was a relief. A waterfall of warmth flooded his chest, lust close behind, when her arms again circled his neck and she pressed her body to his, reaching for his mouth with hers like a lifeline. The taste of her, strong and sweet, grounded him in the moment, making it feel as if he'd last kissed her yesterday, instead of more than a year ago.

He wasn't sure how long they stood there, absorbed in each other, but the mist grew heavier and he spun them, putting her back to the stone, protecting her from the worst of the rain. He wrapped her in the flaps of his dress coat, wishing the moment would never end.

Steam and droplets of water clouded the dark-framed glasses she wore. He pulled them gently from her face, kissing her brow, trying to absorb her warmth, unable to get enough, not when his insides were shaking. Gina's hands were everywhere, traveling from his neck, down his chest and back again, making it hard for him to think.

"I should have told you I was coming."

Her eyes lit with affection, though they were wet. "You should have…but I'm so relieved you're here, in one piece. You get a pass this time." She kissed a flaming trail down his throat, twisted her fingers in the chain of his dog tags at the neck of his shirt. "Can I take you home with me? I only have a few more things to do here before I'm done for the day."

The initial rush of their kiss banked into a steady hum of need that threatened to topple the precarious balancing act he had going on inside his chest. Now that Gina was in his arms, it was difficult to let go. Life was too unpredictable. But he nodded, taking a steadying breath of cool night air and following her back inside to where Carrie stood at the front desk.

"It's nice to have you back in the States, safe and sound, Ben." Carrie grinned. "I could always tell when Gina heard from you, she was even more effervescent than usual. And I swear her Oklahoma accent got stronger too."

Gina cringed, and he frowned, but she laughed it off and patted him on the arm. "Go sit in the lounge, get a drink at the bar. I'll finish up."

He didn't want to let her out of his sight, but he pushed against the urge to come on too strong, too fast. "Sure."

She smiled again then, reached out, and ran her fingers down his chest, like she had to make sure he really stood there, calming some of the tension that prickled on his skin. Then disappeared back into the office and he sat by the bar to wait.

Gina

BACK IN THE safety of her office, Gina took an unsteady breath, trying to release the thirteen-month-old knot of concern that had lodged beneath her breastbone.

Near radio-silent for nearly three weeks, Ben had let her know that he'd arrived back in the States, but little else. A few brief texts. No video calls. She'd begun believing he was done with her. She'd done her role as a supportive, entertaining friend, made him smile a few times. As unpleasant as it was to accept, maybe they both needed to return to regular life on their respective coasts. No harm, no foul.

Pressing a hand against the tumultuous emotions—relief, anger, lust, affection—rioting inside, she tried to get herself under control.

She fought the urge to run to the bar, to latch on and check every part of him, to prove to herself that he was really whole and safe. To tell him all the delicate feelings she'd been shoving under the rug for the past year. Or drag him into one of the empty rooms upstairs. Or slap him for making her doubt the friendship. She couldn't decide which.

None of those things would happen. She wouldn't let them. Here at work, she always kept her head on straight and her impulses in check. Just taking him outside for the kiss, still on the hotel grounds, risked her professional example. Carrie wouldn't say anything, but it was fortunate that her boss had already left for the day. Gina was on the verge of big things here, and she couldn't let her personal life get in the way.

The quiet task of verifying her checklists for the wedding scheduled for the next day settled her. By the time she'd finished and tossed her coat over her arm to return to the lobby, she felt as though she had herself more under control.

Ben stood when she came out of her office, and pride washed over her. He was so handsome, so strong. Clean shaven and crisp in his uniform, so different from the slightly scruffy man in jeans she'd spent hours with in the airport more than a year before.

"Goodnight, Carrie." Gina called to where her friend stood at the front desk in the quiet lobby.

"Goodnight, and congratulations, again. You and Ben should go celebrate. You've earned it." The phone rang and Carrie waved.

"Celebrate?" Ben's hand warmed the small of her back as they walked out into the dark.

"It's not that big a deal. I landed a booking for a big conference and we're signed for three years so..." She felt herself brimming with pride, this time for herself, excited to share the news with him as she explained. The deal was good for the hotel and if she could keep up the good work, might well be worth a pay raise or —better yet—a promotion to the director of events position she coveted.

"That's terrific. You wanted it and got it. Well done." He paused on the sidewalk, grabbed her chin to press a slow, sweet kiss to her lips, making her world tilt, the rich taste of him slowing her blood. "Let me take you out. We'll celebrate."

"Oh, no, sir." Gina's breath came out on a groan of arousal.

"I've waited over a year and there's only one place I want you right now. We can eat anytime. When do you have to leave?"

He pressed his back to the wall, pulling her with him, waiting for a large crowd of rowdy college students to pass on the sidewalk, eyes scanning the street methodically. "I fly back to San Diego the day after tomorrow." Glancing back at her, he held her gaze. "I'm sorry. I wish I had more time."

"Oh." She deflated. "Yeah, me too. I feel like we've hardly talked the last couple of weeks."

He didn't move when the crowd passed, and for the first time Gina noticed the stiffness with which he held his left arm and the bandage peeking out from the edge of his sleeve. "Ben, what are you doing in town, exactly? Besides visiting your old friend Snowflake."

"I was visiting a friend." His familiar frown returned. "At Walter Reed."

"Walter Reed. The military hospital. In DC?" When he moved to walk again, she grabbed his arm, desperate to find out what happened but too afraid to ask.

"Our platoon hit an IED." Ben rubbed his free hand over the back of his neck, closed his eyes briefly. "I got a little burned helping everybody after. One of my guys got hurt pretty bad. Burns, mostly."

Gina wrapped around him before she could think, face pressed to the hollow of his neck, breathing in his scent of woodsy soap and spice.

"Hey, it's all right. I'm fine." But before he could do more than return the hug, she tugged him by his good hand down the street at a jog. "Whoa, what's the rush?"

She blinked away tears, not willing to let emotions get the best of her just yet. Later, sure. But right now, she was on a mission. "You tried to get yourself burned alive being a hero, and we don't have a lot of time. We're dining in tonight."

"Do you want to drive?" He looked into the steady mist of rain.

"No, my car is on the fritz again, so I walked. It's not that far. Plus, parking stinks. We're better off leaving your car here."

He pulled her in close to his side, slowing her steps, tucking her in under his arm. "I could look at it. I'm a good mechanic."

"No, it's not your problem. I'll get to it, eventually." It had been a choice between fixing the car or buying the plane ticket to Dodge for her sister's wedding in June, and family had won out. She wouldn't let Ben put himself out for her and her slow financial recovery problems.

"You're being stubborn. I have the skills you need. Let me help. I owe you."

She stiffened. "Owe me for what?

"Snowflake, you helped me get through that deployment."

"No, I—"

Ben stopped, pulled her in so their noses nearly touched. "You did."

Heart hammering, she forced herself to look, to really see him. Serious, haunted eyes, the slight bump on the bridge of his nose from when he'd broken it during boot camp, a sheen of rain on his skin, powerful jaw ticking. He believed it. And if he could trust her to help, maybe it wouldn't kill her to do the same.

"Okay." She whispered it, pressed her lips to his cheek. "Come on."

They walked the remaining block in silence and she led him into her narrow shotgun-style apartment, hands a little shaky as she put the key in the lock.

When Gina imagined Ben back in her life—more aptly, in her bed—it was a situation where he appeared there magically. She never thought about the lead up to his reappearance or all the complicated feelings that would go along with genuinely caring about him. For the last thirteen months, she'd compartmentalized, put her life in boxes. Work, family, friends—including her sexy pal, Ben. And she went about her business. She'd figured out not too long into their first FaceTime her role as distraction. She represented normalcy, and that was what he needed. So that's what she'd done. Because that was what you do for a friend. And that was the simple thing; what she'd been telling herself they were for months.

Nothing about this was simple, not anymore. If that hadn't been a frying pan to the face when he appeared in the lobby, it was now.

Gina unlocked the door, stepped inside, and removed her coat, emotion and need humming under her skin. She wanted to throw caution to the wind like she had that night in the hotel, this time to prove his safety to herself with his skin on her skin. But they'd waited more than a year. She shouldn't rush the moment now. So, she hung her coat, took his, and did the same.

They stepped into the living room, the growing silence beginning to feel awkward. Ben looked around, eyes landing on the Afghani street-artist painting that he'd sent her for Christmas that hung over the couch. She bit her lip, not quite sure how to proceed as she watched him examine the piece, appreciating the crisp line of the uniform over his broad back and tapered waist.

"Can I get you a drink?"

Head shake.

"A tour? There's not a lot to see."

"No."

"Should we text?" Gina's fingers twisted together, anxious to touch him. This was so messy. What the heck were they doing? "Would that make this feel less awkward?"

He laughed a little, ran his hand over his hair, disturbing the short locks, and finally turned away from the painting to pin her with his gaze.

"Talking with you is great. And I'm happy to talk or text or whatever it is you need. But that's not what I've been thinking about for thirteen months."

A wave of heat rolled through her, swirled low in her belly. "Really? Me either. So, does that mean we should skip dinner for now?"

Ben's eyes darkened. "There's only one thing I need to eat right now."

"Good." A rush of pure lust had her stumbling forward. "Then we're on the same page."

They lunged for each other, lips and teeth smashing together without grace. Gina's body was electric with urgency, the need to be as close to him as humanly possible, making her hands clumsy when she attacked the buttons of his shirt. She gave up halfway through to unclasp his belt while Ben's fingers tangled in her hair, yanking out the clip that held it. They moved together in a desperate, fumbling dance, kicking off shoes and shedding clothing as he backed her into the living room, lips magnetized together.

Her sweater got caught on her earring when he pulled it over her head, and she squeaked, laughed, when Ben growled at the sight of the silky camisole she wore underneath. He carefully extracted the earring and tossed the tangle aside, shed his own shirt, and pulled her back against him.

The warmth of his skin set hers on fire, all the while the persistent sense of relief for his safely pressed tender emotions toward the surface. She had to fight the urge to cry even as her naked hips ground against his in primal need.

Ben's mouth found its way to her neck. "Bedroom?"

"Upstairs, but there's no time..." She moaned when his mouth clamped to her left breast and she renewed her struggle with his pants, finally freeing the snap to push them down. "We'll get there next time."

Hooking his hands under her ass, he lifted, easily supporting her weight, bringing her thighs around his waist and pressing her to the wall.

"Show off." She throbbed under his touch, the ease at which he aroused her a gift. Gina ground against him, her heart threatening to burst out of her chest, wishing this all felt simpler but needing him just the same. She felt him smile against her skin and cupped his powerful jaw, tilted his face to look in his eyes.

"I'm glad you're back, and safe." When they'd kissed earlier, his shoulders had sheltered her from the rain. The sensation now was no different, and she wanted desperately to offer him something back.

Ben's eyes seemed to soften; the affection there unmistakable. "I'm glad to be here with you."

His breath tickled her nose, and she kissed him softly, a heavy warmth suffusing her limbs. "I'm on birth control. And you're the last person I was with, so if we want to go without the condom…" She could rationalize that she hadn't slept with anyone in the last year because she'd focused on work, on maintaining her image, and there was some truth to it. But if she was honest, she simply had wanted no one else.

"You were my last too. Shit, Gina." Ben groaned, the rumble in his chest tickling her nipples. "You can't tell that to a guy who hasn't had sex in more than a year. I already worry about lasting for you."

She laughed, stroked the muscles of his shoulders and neck as he lifted her from the wall and gently transferred them to the sofa.

"I've been thinking about this"—he dropped to his knees and laid kisses from her hip to her pubic bone—"for months." She made a sound of frustration when he evaded her touch. Gina wanted to feel his weight on her, pinning her down, as if that would somehow prove his realness, his presence to the tiny part of herself that still worried this was all a dream. Instead, he divested her of her panties and methodically stroked and licked his way closer to her center until she writhed. That magic tongue went to work, and she nearly laughed.

The speed at which he had her knocking on orgasm's door was comically fast. Shivering with the build-up, his eyes pinned hers, hot and demanding as he added his fingers. And then it was all over; a tidal wave of release smashing through her.

When Gina shattered, Ben crawled up her body like a desperate man. She made room for him, their movements instinctual. And as he filled her, she couldn't help but think that the sex was easier than the tangle of emotions snaking through her chest. He was everywhere, dominating her vision, his scent in her nose, the ridges of his muscles a sculpted work of art against the softness of hers. In her post-orgasm haze, she wanted him even closer, where the line between them blurred.

The bloom of warmth in her chest had her wrapping herself around him, encouraging him to thrust harder, deeper. He whispered her name over and over as they moved, filling her with a fresh wave of pleasure when she watched his face break under the force of his orgasm.

They lay together, boneless, for several minutes. Gina stroked the back of his head where it rested on her chest and down his back, trying to memorize his shape, the play of his muscles.

"I could stay here forever." Ben's voice was muffled. "But I should get off you."

"I don't know. You make a pretty good blanket." She squeezed him with her legs, still wrapped around his hips, swallowing down the thickness in her throat, not ready to break the connection. It would be nice to keep him, to be the kind of woman who could. She liked making him happy, and he made her feel like a queen when she did.

"You're going to get hungry, eventually."

"How much do you think we would have to pay the DoorDash person to bring the food all the way in here, so we don't have to move? Because I'll do it."

He grunted a laugh, levering up, kissing her breast, her collarbone, her lips on the way. "I'll make you dinner."

"I didn't know you could cook."

"My mom made Brian and I learn." He slipped on his boxer briefs, helped her stand. "Said raised us to be good teammates. Cooking, laundry, cleaning. We were all expected to pitch in— even my dad—because we all lived there."

He wandered into her kitchen while Gina slipped up to her room to put on a robe. When she rejoined him, he had the makings of a Greek omelet out and butter in a pan.

"I'm an okay cook—when I don't get distracted and let things burn." She watched him work, quiet and competent, and couldn't help but think of her childhood. "My mom never let my dad cook. I'm not even sure if he can make toast. Very old-school gender roles in that way. The kitchen was her area, and she taught me and Natalie the basics. We always ate dinner on the good plates at six o'clock sharp, when my dad came home from work. And we girls cleaned up."

Ben slipped the omelets onto two plates and set them on the table. "I remember. I joined a few of those dinners."

"That's right. I think I spilled my milk during at least one of those because I was so busy checking you out." She smiled, glad the memory was sweet now, not painful. Because here they were. Ben, a bronzed tactical athlete in his underwear, dwarfing her little kitchen table, eating an omelet. He didn't fit here, but she liked the air pressure better when he was around.

Intent on chewing and staring, Gina jumped when her phone rang, smacking the speaker button on automatically.

"Hi, Mom, it's so nice to hear from you."

Ben leaned back in the chair; expression guarded as he watched her and listened.

"How are you, sweetheart? How is work and all that?"

"I'm fine, Mom. Work is great. Actually, I just signed a major conference. It's a great coup for me." Like always, a part of her hoped for the reaction that soothed all her sore edges, the one that would make all the stretching and binding herself down feel worth it, and as usual, her mother disappointed.

"Oh, dear, do you have to work so much? I still can't believe you didn't make it back for the holidays. It wasn't the same here without you."

Gina softened. "Mom, I'm sorry. But I told you, I couldn't take Christmas and be there for the week of Nat's wedding too. I don't have enough vacation time."

"You work too much." Deborah's voice snapped. "I read that stress raises your cortisol levels and causes weight gain. You don't want to be the chubby bridesmaid, do you? Keep that in mind."

"Jeez, Mom, I—"

"I just want you to be healthy and have security. I want to make sure someone is taking care of you. I can't do that when you're so far away."

There had been plenty of years where her mother's concern for her security and wellness were warranted. The shame of that, knowing how epically she'd failed, had Gina pressing her fingers to her eyes, self-doubt lingering despite the promise of her current job and living situation.

"How is your hair?" Her mother continued. "Are you using that straightening product I sent to tame those wild curls of yours?"

The scrape of the chair on the floor made Gina look up. Ben held her gaze steady, giving her strength and understanding where her mother seemed incapable of it, and a smile twitched her lips. "I shaved my head. No curls to worry about."

"Virginia Abigail Smith, that had better be a joke."

"It is. My hair is fine. The product is fine. Everything is fine."

"Good. Well, I have to go. I just wanted to check in. Love you, dear. Bye!"

Gina took a deep breath when the line went quiet, but the clamor of feelings from the past few hours were too many, and she burst into tears.

"Are you okay?" Ben's eyes widened in panic. "What can I do?"

"Just give me a minute. I can't think."

"Cognition is low when stress is high." Disgust with her mother's attitude obvious, Ben shook his head. "People don't think as clearly when they're stressed, which is why so much of military training is repetition. So thought isn't necessary. Here," he pushed the plate back toward her. "Eat."

Gina hiccupped, appreciating his urge to care for her. "This." She took up the fork and gestured to her face, where tears streamed uncontrollably, nearly poking herself in the eye. "It's a thing I do when I'm stressed. Or really happy. It's this or sex or dying my hair red, but I really don't want to look like Little Orphan Annie."

He nodded, as if it made perfect sense. "Right."

She took a bite and chewed, frowning. "And because you're so stupidly amazing, I wasn't having sex with other people in the last year. So, there have been a lot of tears."

"Why didn't you tell me?" Ben's fingers stroked her wrist, his brows pinched in concern.

"Why would I? It's a coping mechanism." Gina wanted to share with him, wanted him to know he mattered, but her need for self-reliance was important too. "I don't need to put that on you, especially when you had a much more stressful life than me."

"All right." Ben looked at her quietly for a moment, thoughtful. "Do you have a television in your bedroom?"

Gina hiccupped again, ate another bite of omelet, continuing to let the riot of sadness course through her. "Yes."

"Perfect." He waited for her to finish eating, cleaned up the plates, and scooped her up, bridal style, and began carrying her up the stairs toward her bedroom.

"What are you doing?" Gina sniffed, the tears finally slowing.

"The only thing I can think of."

While the main room of the apartment was basic white and gray, her bedroom exploded with personality, part craft studio and collections, part mess. It was a space devoted entirely to herself, the place where she let her creative imagination run wild, and her fingers twitched with nerves over the chain of his dog tags as he crossed the threshold. She glanced at the mosaic of dream catchers she'd woven, the pink wingback chair she'd reupholstered herself, the unkempt piles of fabric next to a small sewing nook, and the usual bedroom laundry chaos. "Don't look too closely. You'll burn your retinas."

He looked around, quickly assessing. "I like it. It's very you."

He climbed on the bed, settled her between his legs, and picked up the remote, quickly pulling up *Annie* and hitting play. "There. Is that better?"

"It's great." She turned her cheek to his chest, loving the way his soothing warmth burned through her back. "But you hate musicals."

"True. But I really like you, and I'd rather fight an entire war alone than have to watch you cry because your mother is self-absorbed."

Tears threatened again, emotion overwhelming. "I really like you too. I mean, I know she just wants the best for me, but she twists it up. It's frustrating to feel successful and never have her see it as enough."

Ben's arms wrapped around her, steady and strong. "You're better than good enough."

Peace soothed her quivering heart, and she tipped her head back onto his chest, humming the intro music when Ben stilled.

"I remember going to one of your plays with Nat. Why didn't you stick with it?"

The peace she'd been feeling evaporated. "I failed out. And then I had some...financial problems. That's why it took me so long to graduate."

He caught her chin with one hand, forcing her to look at him when she would have pulled away, seeing through her evasion. "It hurts you. Tell me."

This was Ben. He wouldn't judge her or mock her or give her a lecture. She knew this conversation would have to happen eventually. That they'd avoided it this long was a minor miracle in itself.

"I partied too hard freshman year and failed out. I was irresponsible. And, I was afraid to tell my parents, so I re-enrolled, taking a class at a time, working at the same time." Gina pressed a hard breath through her teeth, wishing the memory would stop aching. The sense of stupidity.

"And then I met Dustin. He acted in a local theater and did

bits in commercials. I uprooted my life for him and we moved in together. It wasn't love, but he and his friends were fun, and we had the same interests. There was enough attraction to keep it interesting. Four months into our new lease, he disappeared, took off for Hollywood. And I found out he'd opened a credit card in my name, racked up all kinds of charges. None of our supposed friends would help me find him. I got left holding the bag for all of it."

She squeezed her eyes shut, trying to rebury the painful memories, and felt Ben's lips press her temple. The memory still pained her. Not simply being duped, used and discarded, but abandoned as well.

"You've been busting your ass fixing it ever since. I'm sorry, Snowflake. Tell me his name, I'll find him. Introduce him to some Marines."

She opened one eye, huffed out a laugh. "No." But she breathed him in, reminding herself that being with Ben would be easy, which was exactly why she had to be careful. "That's why it's so important to me to have my own place, things on my terms. I—literally—can't afford to count on anyone like that again."

"Not even someone you can trust? With your life?" His fingers brushed her cheek.

Annie was on the screen, singing *Tomorrow* and Gina closed her eyes. "I'm not sure. Maybe someday."

Ben

WEARING A STUPID, satisfied smile on his face, Ben closed the hood of Gina's car with a thump and wiped his hands with a rag before pulling out his phone.

> Ben: I can't get 'little girls' out of my head and it's your fault.

> Snowflake: When you say it that way you sound like a perv

> Ben: Get your mind out of the gutter

> Snowflake: You like me in the gutter. I just realized I missed a perfect opportunity to play naughty nurse with my wounded warrior.

> Ben: Annnnd now that outfit is in my Amazon cart. Overnight delivery.

> Ben: Fixed your car. It was the alternator.

> Snowflake: How?

> Ben: You'd be surprised what you can get when you're in uniform. I borrowed tools from a mechanic at the gas station down the street.

The stupid smile got impossibly wider. Their night together had been soothing, both intimate and comfortable, as if they'd been together that way for years. Now that he understood her experience, things between them could only get better.

He needed this, to help take care of her. Not because Gina couldn't take care of herself, but because they were a good team. He'd slept better with her in his arms than he had in months, only waking to the nightmare of fire once, and she'd soothed him back to sleep with her touch.

He'd been able to fix her car—and she'd let him. And after he cleaned up, he was going to join her at the hotel to crash a wedding and watch her work. He looked forward to seeing that side of her, the sexy, competent, professional woman in charge. If he was lucky, he could corner her in her office after the event for some very unprofessional behavior.

As soon as he got back to San Diego, he would fill out the application for the Force Fitness program. Because if nothing else, the explosion reminded him that life was short. He knew what he and Gina had was more than simple friendship. She would need more time to get used to the idea, but he was going to do his level best to convince her.

Satisfied with the decision, he cleaned up and began the walk over to the hotel.

Boom!

Ben hit the ground and rolled into a crevice against a building before he registered the cracking metallic thump from a dump truck tailgate. It slammed again, and he started, heart racing, sweat blooming on his skin. Scuttling back against the building, he stood slowly, the fiery flashback in front of his eyes making him feel faint.

A couple of pedestrians gave him a wide berth, gazes leery. Blinking away the vision, Ben swore softly. He'd walked right past the construction crew, had seen the dump truck. But his body responded as if still in a war zone.

"Fuck." He took a moment to center himself, trying to pull up the image of Dodge that he'd went through with Gina, but his heart still raced. Her voice helped, though, so he started walking again, reliving the way she'd sung "It's the Hard Knock Life" over breakfast that morning.

By the time he walked into her office at the hotel, though his skin still felt like it was a size too tight, he felt more in control.

"Hey, there you are. Just in time for lunch." Gina stood from her desk and came to meet him for a quick kiss. When she pulled away, her eyes narrowed on him and she reached for his hand. "Are you okay?

"I'm fine." The lie was automatic. Whatever was going on, he'd figure it out. He would protect her from it. "Everything's just fine."

SLEEPLESS NIGHTS IN MAY

GINA

Still wired when she got home from supervising the Anderson-Fletcher wedding, Gina kicked off her shoes. It was half past midnight when she sat in her kitchen with a sparkling water, a block of cheddar, and her phone.

> Snowflake: Hey. What'cha doing?

> Snowflake: I can't sleep. You should entertain me

They'd had to cancel their planned meetup in Denver due to scheduling conflicts, and now they wouldn't see each other until Nat's wedding. Ben had become a fixture in her daily life and having him back in the states, while less worrying, felt like a tease.

> Ben: Just getting back from a run.

Gina glanced at her watch. Usually, Ben was in bed by now. Nine-thirty at night seemed late for a run to her, but then she wasn't a fitness addict like Ben and his buddies. She was happy if she got a spin class a couple times a week.

His face appeared on the screen, sweaty and pale. Concern wound its fingers around her throat.

"Are you okay? Did you run longer or harder than usual?" She wanted to keep it light, but he looked terrible.

"Yeah, maybe. I'm not sure. It usually helps."

"Ben, you're not making sense." Gina's hands went clammy. "A run usually helps? Helps what?"

"I've been having some trouble…since the explosion." His hand shook as he rubbed it over his eyes and sat down. "Sleeping. Nightmares. Fire, mostly. Tonight was a bad one. It's flashback shit. It'll pass. I've had some of this before. After deployments. Not quite this bad but it'll get better."

"You've been dealing with this for months and you never mentioned it to me?" Hurt prickled deep in her chest. They talked every day. Didn't he trust her?

"I didn't want to worry you. I'm sorry." He rubbed his face again and the sound of defeat in his voice snuffed out her spark of anger.

Being mad at him would have been preferable, easier than feeling helpless. The nights they'd been together she'd noticed fretful movements in his sleep, but had thought little of it. Some people were twitchy. "Have you asked for help? Some kind of counseling?"

"It's always worked its way out before. Being with the boys, running and PT, that usually makes it manageable."

"But, Ben. You might need more than that this time." It sounded like PTSD. "You went through something traumatic."

"It'll fade away." He closed his eyes. "Mostly, I just wish you were here. Nothing hurts when I'm holding you."

The statement was simultaneously flattering and frightening. Being a comfort was one thing. But she'd never been important to anyone the way he described, felt ill suited to the responsibility.

"I'm not sure what to do. Do you want to do the relaxation technique, the happy place thing? Walk through Dodge again?"

"What I think about when I need to be happy is you, not Dodge. Listening to your voice."

Suddenly, Gina's head ached. He was supposed to be the strong one. Half the time she felt like her life was held together with duct tape and a smile. "That's beautiful, but it scares me too. I want to help, but it also feels unfair, to put that on me. I can't save you or find your answers. Half the time, I can barely take care of myself and my own baggage. You need to get help. There are professionals for that."

"That's bullshit. A shrink doesn't know me like you do. And I don't expect you to fix me. I'm not fucking broken just…a little messed up at the moment. Being with you feels right. I didn't mention it before because I didn't want you to have to deal with it." Ben's brows furrowed and his eyes bored right through the screen at her. "And you've been taking care of yourself very well, for a long time. Don't cut yourself down like that. Who are you trying to convince you're not good enough? Me or yourself?"

Gina blinked back tears. Now, they were both breathing hard, both hurt and angry. It was the first time they'd ever fought for real. And it made her feel sick, like standing on a ship in a stormy sea.

"Okay. We're both tired. Let's start over." She leaned back, took several deep breaths, and watched his nostrils flare, doing the same. "I want you to be okay. I want to help. And I've always been an excellent distraction, so let me distract you."

She told him about the wedding that night, where two groomsmen had hit on the bride's very attractive and single mother, and dirty-danced with her during the reception. They then got in a fistfight, only to be hauled off by their collars and thrown into the street by the groom.

"Weddings. They are never boring." Gina was glad to see Ben's face soften with her story, more relaxed. "Do you know yet if you'll make it to Nat's wedding next month?" She knew Ben was a mission-oriented kind of guy. He would likely feel better, more centered, if he had a goal in his sights. "We'll get some time together. You can help me play the part of a successful professional in front of my parents. Help keep me sane. It'll be a fair trade."

"You don't need help with that. It's not an act. But I'd happily be your date."

"I feel like that would create questions about our relationship that I don't know if I can answer. Not yet. If I show up with you, my mother will reserve the church and print invitations before we leave the reception." She tried to keep it light, the security of her goals and the rules for attaining them threatening to crack at the foundation. Somewhere along the line, they'd gotten in deep with each other, and she'd only just realized it.

"Would it be terrible for people to think we're together? Look at us." Ben immobilized her with his dark green eyes. "Doesn't it feel like we're together already?"

"You know how hard it is for me in Dodge." He was important to her and she wouldn't lie to herself about that. But presenting it at the wedding? "We have a thing, yes. And it's good. But I don't want my mother or the small army of gossiping nitpickers in our hometown to attack it. Not yet. It's too good. Come on, Ben." She smiled impishly, relieved that the hurt had left his face. "Will you sneak around with me?

DODGE PARTNERS IN JUNE

GINA

"One more, big smiles. That's perfect."

Gina loosened her jaw when the photographer finished, trying to release the tension that screamed from her eyelids to her toes. Prolonged exposure to her family was a migraine waiting to happen, from her mother's little digs about the fit of the bridesmaid dress to the quality of the gift she'd given her sister and Adam. And then there was the five-minute rant she'd gone on after Gina hadn't cleaned up after her father during breakfast that morning. In her mother's mind, expecting a grown man to clean up after himself was tantamount to resigning her ovaries.

The only saving grace of the weekend was Ben.

With a more natural smile, she remembered seeing him before the ceremony, so handsome in the dress blues uniform that he'd worn per Natalie's request. The sight had taken her breath away. They'd snuck off for a laugh-filled quickie, struggling to be inconspicuous in the cornfield behind the church, both feeling like a couple of horny teenagers.

As soon as her bridesmaid duties were over, she'd drag him off behind one of the giant rosebushes. She longed to feel Ben's fingers slip over the thin blue fabric again, setting fire to her skin, pulling her against his hard body, holding her up so that she didn't have to stand on her own.

"Wake up, dream girl. I want a couple more with just my little sister." Natalie, the quintessential glowing bride, waved her bouquet and waited for the other bridesmaid minions to adjust the fall of her train. Gina took a deep breath and told herself that the discomfort of the weekend was worth it for Nat. She was truly glad for her sister.

"You know, you were a pretty obnoxious bride during the planning process. And I know from firsthand experience how bad that can get—but you did good, sis." Gina bumped her sister's shoulder gently with her own when the photographer got the shots she wanted. "The wedding's beautiful. You're beautiful. And I'm thrilled for you and Adam."

"Wow, a compliment was in there somewhere, I think." Nat smiled. "Adam's very patient with me. I made the poor man crazy, but he worships me and I love him, so it'll work out."

Gina struggled against the sarcastic remark that wanted to fly out of her mouth. "Good. So...are you going to keep working? Or become a socialite housewife like Mom?"

Natalie's eyes narrowed. "Why do you do that? I am going to keep working. I love being a real estate agent. And, yes, I may cut back when we have kids or take on different—so called socialite-type activities. But if I do, it's because that's I want, and what's best for us. Adam's my husband, not my owner." She lowered her voice, "I'm not Mom. And Adam isn't our dad. Just because that's where you and I came from doesn't mean we're destined for it."

Ashamed, Gina fiddled with the sash of her dress. "I know, I'm sorry. You're right." She was. But intellectually knowing what marriage could be, versus what she'd grown up seeing, was a difficult link to break.

"I know being here is hard for you, and you have this whole other life back east that's better than what you ever had here. But we're your family." Nat looked her directly in the eye. "And we love you too, warts and all. Don't forget that."

"I know." Gina blinked hard, emotion flooding her frustration, and she reached to hug her sister fiercely. "I'm sorry it's this way. I love you too."

Nat's arms squeezed, soothed. "I know. Now let me go. You're going to ruin my makeup."

Wiping her damp cheeks with a huff, Gina stepped back. She didn't give her sister enough credit. It was easy to be critical of her, of the town, especially from afar. But she realized that criticism might say more about her own insecurities than it did their actual shortcomings.

By the time the band leader announced the bridal party, she felt steadier. When she caught Ben's eye across the crowded lawn, saw the barest hint of a smile on his lips, she knew it was for her. With just a look, he made her feel simultaneously sane again and hot all over.

Gina's heart fluttered dangerously, and she clamped down on the unpredictable sensation.

Grabbing a glass of champagne from a waiter's tray before she could overthink things, she meandered her way in Ben's direction. He stood with his parents and a loose group of locals. She took a couple minutes to find her way over inconspicuously, stopping periodically to make benign small talk with other guests.

When she finally approached, she caught the tail end of the Ben Richardson fan club fawning over the ribbons on his chest. She bit back a smile at the discomfort evidenced in the white-knuckle grip he had on his glass of whiskey. Their eyes locked for a beat, and she could practically hear him screaming for escape.

"That's real impressive, Ben." Jenkin Baker took a slug from his beer bottle, glancing in Gina's direction with a smarmy smile. "Workin' on anything special right now?"

Seeing it, Ben's eyes narrowed fractionally. "I'm studying for my next promotion, to Staff Sergeant."

"How's that going?" Gina pointed her glass in his direction, enjoying playing the role of ignorant acquaintance.

"Better than high school."

She held back a laugh at his response. The week before, via FaceTime, she'd helped him run through review questions strip-study style. Ended up in her panties and one sock, and had learned a few things about the military. "I thought you were a good student."

"Mediocre." Ben seared her with his green eyes. "I'm better with my hands."

She snorted, nearly spewing wine. "Excuse me, wrong pipe." Bonnie patted her on the back and Gina smiled behind her glass as she got herself under control.

"So, when are you getting out?" Jenkin asked. "Gonna come back and take over the ranch with your brother?"

"I've got a few more years on my contract. Then…we'll see." Ben's gaze lingered on Gina, his words pitching something uncomfortable through her belly. "I've been accepted to the Marine Force Fitness Instructor program. That'll take me out of the fleet for a couple of years. Offers a more normal schedule."

He'd mentioned an application to the FFI program before, but this was the first she knew about his acceptance. Or what it might mean for his future. Questions pushed against her lips, but she bit down, knowing now wasn't the time.

"You really ought to settle down. Let some nice woman take care of you." Jenkin's wife, Barb, pinched Ben's cheek as if he were a small boy. "Start a family."

Before he could respond, Gina jumped in, needing to reset the balance that flipped inside her. "Yeah, Ben. Are you seeing anyone? A big handsome guy like you…seems like you'd have women begging to become barefoot and pregnant."

"Careful, Ginny. Your romantic streak is showing." Ben's deadpan response had the rest of the group snickering. "Actually, I'm seeing an amazing woman. She's smart, kind, generous. Very successful in her job. A little impulsive, but that just keeps her interesting."

Her mouth went dry, and she took a long sip of wine.

"When do we get to meet her?" Brian held a small appetizer

plate in his hands, ate a cheese cube, and continued. "Hell, it doesn't seem that long ago we all figured you'd be marrying a Smith."

"There's still time." Ben stole an olive off his brother's plate and popped it in his mouth, ignoring the confused look on the faces of the circle. Gina's face heated, not quite sure if she should be amused or pissed.

Bonnie held back a smile. "Speaking of Smiths, Gina. You should come over for dinner with the family tomorrow. I'd love to hear all about your work at the hotel. How long are you in town?"

"Day after tomorrow." Ben and she said in unison.

"Right," Bonnie said smoothly, as if it was totally natural for Ben to know. "We'll talk about it later. It sure is great having my oldest back home." She slipped an arm around his waist and squeezed. "We're proud but we miss him bunches when he's gone."

Ben brushed a kiss on his mother's temple. "It's good to be here, Mom."

The differences between her family experience and Ben's couldn't have been more obvious in that moment. He loved them, they enjoyed being together, while she could barely stand her own. Throat tight with the sense of failure, Gina reminded herself that she'd never be able to be here in Dodge, not happily. Could Ben be happy anywhere else? She cared too much about him to make that demand.

"...I ran into Dr. Chris getting a drink." Bonnie said when Gina tuned back into the conversation. "He thinks he can get me in for the knee replacement in October. We'll be all done harvesting by then, but I'll be down for at least a month, if not two. Think you can make it down to give us a hand? Even for a bit?"

"I'll do what I can."

"We'll get through it, Bonnie-girl." Ben's dad rested a hand on her shoulder. "You'll be running circles around us again before you know it."

Though she could feel Ben's questioning eyes on her, Gina politely excused herself, needing a minute to reset. She retreated to the iron bench behind the garden shed. Looking over rows of purple coneflower, she stared into the hayfield beyond, trying to settle her jumble of emotions.

A few minutes later, Ben came around the corner.

"Hey." He sat down next to her, handing her a fork for the slice of cake he held. "Pretty wedding."

"It is. Thanks for being here." She leaned into him, absorbing his steady strength, allowing it to soothe her raw edges.

He forked some cake and held it to her mouth. "Something about my family that upsets you? You took off."

Gina took the cake plate from his hand to steal more. "Not upsetting, exactly. I just see how easy you all are together. I'm the odd duck in my family. Nat and I get on okay, but I'll never be close with my parents. I love them, but it's never going to be easy."

"I got lucky with the parent lottery. I'm sorry it hurts you."

"It's fine." She didn't need to burden him with it. Not today.

Gina watched when he went to lick a bit of frosting off his thumb and grabbed his wrist to lick it herself, her fingers dancing across the delicately healed scars on his skin. His eyes dilated, and a thrill ran up her spine when he scooped the back of her neck and pulled her in for a kiss that tasted like sugar.

Lips tangled, wild and hot, and the cake hit the ground. Before she knew it, she was straddling his lap and wearing his white uniform cover on her head, while his hands ran up under her skirt to stroke her thighs.

"Shit." He kissed a trail up her collarbone. "I'm suddenly wishing I was an exhibitionist."

She laughed, warmth suffusing her limbs as she ground against him. "You know, I came over here feeling pleasantly depressed and bitchy, and now you've turned me upside down." She pressed her forehead to his while the afternoon sun heated her back. "You're good at that, making me look at things differently than I did before. It's really annoying." Gina kissed him, soft and slow, memorizing the shape of his lips with hers. "I like having you around to lower my anxiety. Especially when my mom is nearby."

Ben's thumb brushed over her chin. "You lower my anxiety, too. And…I guess now's as good a time as any to tell you I started seeing a counselor a couple weeks ago. Greer and I both, actually. Things are getting better. Thanks for pushing me on that."

Opening her eyes, she saw the vulnerability in his face. She traced the line of his jaw and chin with her fingertips, wishing she could do something, anything, to make it easier. "Good. I want to be there for you, to help, but I didn't know how. I just want you to be happy."

"I am. Especially when we're together. Gina." Ben locked his eyes with hers. "I'm in love with you."

Her heart swelled and the shell she'd built around it cracked, but resisted breaking. He must have sensed her tension, because his hands came from under her skirt to wrap around her waist.

"I'm not asking you for anything. Not pushing. I just want to be on record because it's true. I told you once I want what my parents have. A real partnership. I think we could have that if we both tried. When you have something good sitting in front of you, you grab it and never let go. Life is too short." He closed his eyes for a beat. "Too short not to go for it when it's there."

"Ben, I…" She kissed him again, wanting to just let go. "I don't disagree. But…"

"But." The weight of his sigh was a wave.

"But. I made a career out of grabbing—or stealing, or drinking, or moving or proposing—without thinking things through for almost a decade. And I'm still paying for it." She took a deep breath, trying to stay calm. "You said you were patient, and I need you to be patient right now. We live three thousand miles apart. I'm focused on my career. I know that my experience with Dustin screwed me up, but I have a solid, secure life now. If you and I commit to each other, one of us is going to be uprooted. I'm not willing to do that, not now. And I'm not willing to ask you to do it either."

She needed to be completely honest. With him and herself. Gina's hands shook, love and fear tangling together inside her, alongside a tiny seed of hope. "I love you too. I do."

Her fingertips covered his lips when he would have spoken. "But when Dustin left me, he stole more than just my identity and my money. I lost the ability to trust myself too, and I'm still earning that back. I have the self-control not to go streak through this wedding, or shoplift Kit-Kats. I've grown out of that. But with big decisions, especially that rely on someone else...I need more time. I need to be sure."

The recklessness that had seemed like such a fun part of Dustin's personality had turned out to be a fire that burned all the relationships around them. When he left, she'd been truly alone. "My work at Davidson has given me security and a kind of family. I can do so much there, be something I'm proud of and I refuse to walk away from that."

"I get that you have goals and would never ask you to give them up." Ben's voice was low and fierce, but his hands remained gentle, stroking her skin. "I can transfer units. I can finish my contract time and get out, get a government job if I want, finish my twenty years. Or back to school. I need to figure it out, and I'm trying." His jaw worked. "I know I need something, a goal, that isn't you. But that doesn't mean I'm wrong for wanting you, for wanting us."

"You're not wrong for wanting." Gina took his cover off her head, gently ran her fingers over the brim before carefully placing it back on his, wishing she had his confidence, that he could understand her resistance had nothing to do with him and everything to do with her. "And I'm not wrong for needing you to wait."

"Shit, Snowflake. Why are we putting the cart before the horse? We made it a year in different countries." Ben's familiar frown and determined gaze lifted something inside her. "We have something good between us. Let's just try. For the rest of the year, at least. Please?"

Hope pushed against the doubts in Gina's mind, Ben's steady pulse under her palm, crowding them out with persistence.

"There's a conference I'd like to attend in September. My boss wants to send me or Carrie. I can convince her I should go." Gina took a breath. "It's in San Diego." A smile curved on her face, growing impossibly wide when Ben grinned like a kid at Christmas.

"The FFI is at Quantico, in Virginia, for six weeks. I'm scheduled to go mid-October. We could have weekends together. And…the Marine Corps Ball is in November. I could take you."

"Does that mean I get to wear a beautiful princess dress? And you'll dance with me?"

"I don't know." Warmth ignited on her skin when Ben traced a curl on her cheek. "Depends on if I get to feel you up under your fancy dress."

She cupped his face. "It's a deal, partner."

VIEWS OF THE BAY IN SEPTEMBER

BEN

*B*en watched as Gina stepped out the back door of the convention center event room from the *Hospitality Experts* cocktail party, and made her way down the stairs toward him, plastic badge jangling around her neck. As usual, twin bolts of lust and affection shot through him, and when she dumped her cultured business stride to launch into his arms, knocking him back into the railing, he felt like the luckiest man in the world.

"Shit, Gina." He laughed, their mouths meeting unerringly, her scent wrapping around him. Seeing her was always such a huge relief, as if whenever they were apart, he held his breath. She was air, and he'd been holding tight for so long that he'd nearly forgotten how to inhale. "I missed you."

They'd tried to meet twice in the months since the wedding,

but between her work schedule, cost, and his limited leave, they hadn't managed more than their usual texting and FaceTime calls.

"I missed you too."

They drank each other in while the cool breeze off the water teased the ends of her hair, tangling in his fingers.

"We have to stop." Ben finally pulled away, nipped her lower lip, dragged his hands over the softness of her ass, his hands failing to follow direction. "Or I'm going to end up doing something very indecent in a very public place." He took her hand, leading her down the stairs. "Plus, we have a date."

"A date?"

"You know the family I was born to." They reached the bottom of the stairs and began walking along the marina. "Now it's time for you to meet my Marine brothers. In person." His stomach squeezed, excitement and nerves in equal measure, knowing the boys were bound to do something embarrassing. "Ryan and Greer. Hodges is supposed to come too, but he just got a new bike and he's probably halfway to Las Vegas right now."

She pressed her cheek to his arm as they walked. "That means a lot. I know they're important to you."

That was an understatement. He couldn't put into words how much they'd been through together, or how much it meant to have each other to commiserate with.

"Have you looked over the conference schedule yet? I'd like to take you around, do the tourist thing while you're here. The beach, the Midway, Balboa Park. Or I could take you up the coast, closer to my usual neck of the woods."

"Those would all be wonderful, really. But I shouldn't miss too much of the events at the conference. I'm trying to make an impression, network. I'll have a couple of evenings free, like tonight. Not much during the day. You know, with what I learn here, I think I'm this close." She held her thumb and finger an inch apart. "This close to getting the director promotion."

"That would be excellent." But disappointment was a stone in his gut. "I thought you were going to try and stay an extra day?"

"I really can't. Carrie's covering for me. But…" She bit her lip. "I could probably skip the afternoon meetings on Sunday? A few extra hours together?" Her arms wrapped more firmly around his. "I've heard great things about the beaches here."

"Sure," he linked his hand with hers, wishing things were a little different. But this was fucking love, and he wasn't about to whine about limited time. It was already more than other people got.

They strolled along the walkway, hands linked, intent on people-watching and enjoying the tail end of the sunset light show streaking out over the water. Like a genuine couple, Ben thought. And it felt good.

When they reached the restaurant, he put his hand on the door but didn't open it. "Are you ready for this?"

"Ben, come on."

"I'm serious. These are battle-tested warriors you're about to meet. One is so pretty he's been on Marine billboards and the other could charm the pants off a nun. I'll let you decide who's who. You love me, right?"

Laughter bubbled from her mouth. "Yes, I love you, you ridiculous man. Open the door and feed me tacos. I promise not to jump your friends."

"Truth?" He kept his face serious, but the smile came through in his voice.

She grabbed his face and kissed him hard. "Honest truth!"

"All right." He opened the door and held it, much to the relief of the patrons who he'd blocked from escape on the other side.

Surprised when he got to their table and the others hadn't arrived, Ben checked his phone, but there were no messages. No problem. They'd probably be here any minute. Parking downtown could be a bitch.

He told himself to chill, but his knee bounced under the table and he sent Ryan a quick WTF text. A Marine who wasn't fifteen minutes early was already late.

"I will say Greer and Ryan are the exception, but generally

when Marines get together, especially once the drinking starts, don't take anything they say too seriously. I trust every one of them with my life, but they're a bunch of macho dumbasses. So, keep that in mind."

Amusement dancing in her eyes, she nodded sagely. They were still alone a few minutes later. By the time the waiter came to take their drink order, Ben was about ready to come out of his skin. Gina snagged a chip from the basket the waiter had brought and eyed him curiously. "What's the problem?"

"Nothing." He brushed a finger across the faint freckles on her nose. God, he loved her. "I'm glad you're here."

"I'm sure that's true. And I'm glad to be here too." She placed a hand on his bouncing knee. "But you're vibrating the table and I have never seen you straight antsy like this. Ever. Is the fact that the guys aren't here yet a problem?"

"No, I'm sure they just got hung up." He couldn't have explained why the delay ate at him so much. He didn't need their approval for Gina, or hers for them, but that didn't mean he didn't want it. They'd get here eventually, but a root of worry tried to grow. "It's just..." He reached for her hand. "There's the family you're born with and then there's the family you make. These guys are my family and now, so are you."

"It's important. They're important. I get it." She leaned forward, pressed her lips gently to his, soothing. "Give them a few more minutes. Then start a harassment level number of texts. That's what I do with Andrea. She's always late."

"Aww, look at the lovebirds. Already making a nest." A deep voice boomed over his shoulder.

Absurd relief poured through him at the sound of Ryan's voice. Running a hand through his hair, Ben refreshed the introductions. "Hey, where the hell have you guys been?"

"I had to take a phone call. Hi." Ryan leaned in smoothly to shake Gina's hand and kiss her cheek. "Nice to meet you in person, finally."

Not to be outdone, Greer pulled her in for a friendly hug. "You're much too beautiful to be with Richardson."

Gina glowed with their attention, then turned in his direction and raised an eyebrow at him as she tried to determine who was who in his earlier description of the guys.

After they settled, she skimmed the menu. "Everything's so expensive here. At least everywhere I've been so far."

"I want a margarita the size of my head." Greer shrugged muscular shoulders, glanced at his menu, then tossed it aside. He always got chimichangas. "Big city money, then you add the California tourism prices on top to a place like this?" He hooked a thumb toward the sparkling lights over the bay just beyond their table. "With this view? Twenty, at least for a drink. A million for a tiny shoebox apartment."

"You're not exactly selling her on the city." Ben raised his eyebrows meaningfully. Not that he expected Gina to move here, given her dedication to her life in Wilmington. But if she was interested, he'd encourage it.

"You're here for a work convention?" Ryan gave Greer a meaningful look, sat forward to lean on the table, comically dwarfing his chair.

"Yes, it's a lot of networking with other hospitality and event directors. I'm on the edge of a promotion at work and hoping something I learn here will tip the scales." She glanced at Ben, leaning into the hand that he'd set on the back of her chair. "Plus, it's a good excuse to spend time with this guy."

"I'm glad you came. We were thinking you were a figment of Ben's imagination. Or a hired actress." Ryan smacked Greer on the arm. "See, man? This is called a long-term re-la-tion-ship. Ever heard of it?"

"I have relationships. They just have one-night expirations so that as many women as possible get the opportunity." Greer grinned, deep dimples flashing, and took a little bow. "It's a public service, what I do."

"Jesus, you idiots." Ben flushed with embarrassment, but not sure why. Greer certainly wasn't. And when Gina laughed, amusement twinkling, he felt himself relax a little more.

She put her hand on his thigh and squeezed, as if she knew he needed the connection. "Talk to me about this fitness instructor thing."

"A few years ago, the Navy and Marines realized they'd have better fitness results if they used more education-based instruction, injury prevention, and health maintenance. They started the Force Fitness program as a result." Ryan paused when their drinks arrived. "Daily it means leading training, runs, lifting, recovery, things like that. If you're in long enough, it involves advising PT instructors on fitness programs and coaching."

"I just got accepted to the program too." Greer took a sip from his fishbowl-sized margarita. "Hopefully we all end up staying here, and the Marines don't send me to Guam or wherever the hell."

"They could send you to Guam?" Gina's eyebrows hit her hairline.

Ben let out a frustrated breath, beginning to believe that having her meet these two was a terrible idea. "I mean, technically yes…"

"Even with this new job, you could get moved or have to leave for training or whatever, with no control over where or when? I thought you said it was a more stable position?" Her eyes narrowed and she took a long sip of her margarita.

"The hours are stable. Most weekends off. No deployments," Ryan said.

"But no." Ben tried not to grind his teeth in frustration. This wasn't landing the way it should. He could see it in the flush of her cheeks. "I don't get to say where."

"That doesn't exactly inspire me with confidence. You're saying if I got an amazing job out here tomorrow, you might get sent off to east nowhere before I'd even unpacked my bags? Thank you, no."

"Well." Ben felt the weight of the roadblock she'd dropped,

knowing he should've seen it coming. Desperately wanting her to want this as badly as he did, beginning to doubt she could with all the obvious obstacles. "That clears up any potential questions about you possibly moving here."

"I don't say it to be harsh." Gina's cool fingers stroked the inside of his wrist, and Ben tried to take it as comfort. She leaned in to his ear and lowered his voice. "That unreliability… It's exactly why I promised myself that no man would determine my future again. My life and work and friends are all in Delaware." Ben's gut clenched with the matter-of-fact nature of her words. "I love you, but you're going to have to work around that."

He nodded and she sat back, letting more casual conversation pick back up. When she excused herself to go to the bathroom a minute later, Ben watched her walk away, felt the gazes of his friends on him. "What?"

"Fuck, man." Greer shook his head.

"I gotta say, three thousand miles is a long way to go for a booty call." Ryan popped a chip into his mouth, his stare deliberately bored.

"Don't bait me, asshole." Ben picked up his bottle of Corona. Put it back down. "Look, I'm trying to be patient for her. Someday I'm going to marry that girl and you're going to be in the wedding. I don't want to have to explain to people that your formerly pretty face got jacked up because you insulted my wife."

"You sure about that?" Ryan picked up his beer. "She's got a lot of rules."

"She's independent. For reasons." Ben looked out onto the bay where the lights of a military police boat raced by in the darkness. "But what it comes down to is, she's afraid to lean on me."

"Isn't that a good thing?" Greer licked some salt off the edge of the glass. Ryan rolled his eyes, mumbling, "that drink should come with a shot of testosterone," but Greer ignored him. "Then she's got her own shit. Isn't harping on you all the time?"

"Yeah, to an extent." Ben thought about how his parents managed, sharing decisions, splitting the workload. Trusting each other. He and Gina weren't there yet. He sure as hell hoped their time together next month would help sort it out.

"By the way, I didn't want to mention it with Gina here, but the call I got? That held us up?" Ryan's eyes had gone serious. "It was Mitchell's girlfriend. He's back in the ICU. Some kind of complication from the last grafting surgery. Infection, I guess. It's not good."

Ben pressed fingers to his eyes, forced himself to breathe out slow when the image of Mitchell's burned arm flashed into his brain, smoke billowing from the Humvee. They'd done the best they could. The weight of concern pressed down, but the icy panic that sometimes came from remembering the explosion didn't appear. It was progress. Now all he could do was hope for the best for Mitchell. "That sucks. I'll reach out to him. Thanks for letting me know."

When Gina returned to the table, the guys shared funny stories in an effort to lift the mood. And it worked. By the time they finished eating and made their way outside to the sidewalk, Ben had let go of most of the tension from earlier.

"What are we doing now?" Greer asked, always ready for a party. "Bar? Club? Karaoke?"

"I love karaoke." Gina grabbed Ben's hands and belted an extra twangy version of the country hit "Before He Cheats."

"No, no, no. Make it stop!" Ben made a grab for her, but she danced away, laughing, and he turned back to the guys. "We're done with you two. It's time for the adults to have private time. As soon as I—" He made another grab for Gina, this time hooking her and pulling her in to muffle her voice against his chest. "There we go."

Ryan grinned. "All right, brother. Good luck with that."

Greer slapped him on the shoulder. "Think you're going to need it."

They exchanged goodbyes, Gina continuing to hum the song as they walked, latching onto Ben's arm.

"Don't be surprised if my ears spontaneously combust."

"Worth it." She giggled, pressed a quick kiss to his jaw. "I like your friends."

"I'm glad." A little more of the twist inside him loosened. "I think they liked you too."

As they passed the entrance of an upscale wine bar, an older couple stepped out of the doors and into their path.

"Oh, Virginia, nice to see you again. Enjoying your evening so far? My wife, Beverly, and I were just sampling some excellent cabernets." The man smiled pleasantly.

"I am, thank you. That sounds wonderful. Maybe we'll partake. Jerome, I'm sorry, where are my manners?" Gina gestured to him stiffly. "Jerome Washington is the manager of a boutique hotel in New Orleans. Jerome, this is Ben Richardson."

"Sir." Ben shook his hand, noted its firmness, and Gina's sudden improvement in posture and precise language. Something about the change prompted annoyance. He turned and repeated the process with the sharply dressed Beverly.

"You should. But not too much." Jerome winked. "I expect to see you at the conference bright and early tomorrow. I want to hear all about your ideas on that art exchange program you were mentioning."

"Of course. I'll be there."

They said their goodnights and stood while Jerome and Beverly walked away.

"Your transition is smooth, very impressive." Ben started walking again. "Into professional mode."

"It has to be. What about you with your 'yes sir and ma'am'? Your military training is hardwired."

"You're right." He couldn't fault her for having a professional persona, but wondered when she would learn to trust herself, to be herself, all the time. Ben blew out a breath, not wanting for the conversation to turn into an argument when they had so little time together. Not when life was so fickle. He laced his fingers with hers, pulling her into a shadowed alcove by the seawall. "You default to professional mode. And I have to say"—he dropped his voice, brushed his lips across her ear—"that there is something very sexy about the proper Miss Virginia Smith."

He felt her lips curve against his neck. "Is that right, Sergeant Richardson?"

"Excuse me, ma'am. That's Staff Sergeant Richardson."

She pulled back to look at his face. "You got the promotion?"

The pride and happiness on her face was absurdly satisfying. "I did. And now it's time to get back to your room to celebrate."

"Is that an order, Staff Sergeant?" Her eyes blazed with arousal and she brushed the tips of her breasts against his chest, sending a shuddering breath through them both.

"It is."

They took off down the sidewalk, Ben nearly dragging her, lust and anticipation rushing through his veins. When they got into her hotel room, Gina tossed her purse and badge onto the small desk and grinned naughtily. "What was it you wanted, Staff Sergeant?"

Ben's mouth went dry as she pulled the clasp out of her hair and shook it loose over her shoulders. "I want you."

"Hmmm…" She slipped the light sweater she wore off and reached for the hem of her shirt, giving him a tantalizing hint of skin. "How do you want me?"

"Miss Smith, I'm going to need you to remove your clothes." His cock had already gone rigid, and he put his hands on his hips just to keep from reaching for her. "And put your hands on the glass."

Surprise and excitement flickered across her face, but she complied, slowly removing her top, then stepping out of her skirt, and finally her undergarments, each item sending more of Ben's blood rushing south. "Like this, sir?" And she turned to press her hands to the large paned window that overlooked the San Diego Bay.

Releasing a groan, Ben pressed against her bare body before he could think. "Yes, ma'am." The bay at night was a scatter of shimmering lights and beyond, from Coronado. Looking down from the twentieth floor, the people walking down the Embarcadero were just shadowy miniatures fading in and out of the golden pools of light along the marina. Ben barely registered them. He was too busy losing himself in her, his hands roaming the softness of her breasts, his mouth scraping her neck, desperate for her taste.

When his fingers found her damp arousal and her hips bucked, Ben felt drunk on power. He flicked his thumb over her sensitive bundle of nerves, and she shivered.

"Oh, god, Ben."

He laughed softly. "We're back to Ben now, are we?"

Turning her around, he let her strip off his shirt before he lifted and pressed her back to the cool window, silencing her squeal of surprise with a deep kiss. A kiss that turned rough and demanding, scraping the quiet places inside him where she'd always soothed. Reminding him he lived. Finding her heat again, Ben tormented her clit until she shook.

"Ben, please. I need you. Now."

Pausing long enough to unhook his pants and let them fall to the floor, Ben pressed his throbbing erection inside her slickness, reveling in the tight pulse. It was an exercise in painful pleasure that had them both sighing. He thrust, overwhelmed by sensation, at how she made him feel. "I love you, so fucking much."

She dragged his mouth from her breast back to her lips. "I love you too."

He groaned, the words setting off the electric pressure at the base of his spine. Ben thrust harder, grinding his hips against her center until she cried out, clenching around him and setting off his release. With her limp against him, Ben surged deeper, one hand pressed against the glass, almost lightheaded with the intensity as he emptied himself inside her.

With her body wrapped in his arms, Ben rested his chin on her head, breathing her in, looking out the window over the bay, wondering if there could be a more perfect moment.

SEMPER FIDELIS: ALWAYS FAITHFUL IN NOVEMBER

GINA

The last six weeks had been amazing. And still something inside Gina refused to settle, to trust herself and simply enjoy what she and Ben had together.

Andrea finished placing the narrow gold clip in Gina's hair, holding the long sweep of curls back from her face on one side. "You're going to knock Ben on his ass."

"That's the idea." But she wasn't sure. Gina looked in the mirror, imagining herself at the ball.

Hello. I'm Gina Smith, Staff Sergeant Richardson's friend.

No.

Nice to meet you. I'm Gina Smith, Staff Sergeant Richardson's girlfriend.

Manageable. Not a label she loved but friend was so lame.

Hello, I'm Gina Richardson, Staff Sergeant Richardson's wife.

That felt right. Uncomfortable, difficult, but right. What if it could be as simple as that? As trusting herself. But if it was then why, after all these months, couldn't she tell?

They'd had all but one weekend together since he'd been at Quantico for the FFI training—when he'd had to make a quick trip back to Dodge to see his mother after her knee surgery, but that hadn't upset her. He was a loyal, loving son, and she was glad.

He was nothing like Dustin. She knew that in her heart. But her head couldn't quite let go of all the what ifs.

Ben made her laugh, serviced her car, and helped with the dishes. He made the three-hour drive from Quantico to Wilmington every Friday, arriving with a grumpy little smile every time, just for her. He let her steal the blankets, and hog the shower spray, and he made her feel beautiful and dirty and alive, all at the same time.

Still, the next step seemed too big. She couldn't stop questioning herself. Would he get sick of her having to work late for events? Of indulging her addiction to musicals? Would he get stationed north of nowhere and expect her leave her life go with him? What if he got deployed again and injured, or worse yet, killed? She didn't know if she could survive it. And even if he left the Marines, retired, she couldn't help but wonder if her ability to make him smile would be enough. If she could be enough to keep him.

But he'd wanted to try for the year, and the end was coming fast. How long would he be willing to wait for her to find her courage?

Pressure squeezed along her ribs that had nothing to do with the structure of her dress.

"You look beautiful, Ms. Gina." One of Carrie's twins, Viv, came up beside her aunt with a blue lollipop in her mouth. "Just like Elsa. I was Elsa for Halloween, like, three years in a row."

"Thanks, kiddo." Gina put on a smile and stood, smoothing down the satin seafoam blue dress. With its daring slit and sparkling beadwork at the bodice, she felt like a sexy ice princess, and when she'd tried the dress on for the first time, had only just resisted breaking into song.

Carrie popped her head in the office. "Viv, are you staying out of the way? Your dad's going to be here to pick you and Lena up in just a minute."

"Mom, I'm thirteen, not a baby." Viv gave a monster eye roll and wandered past her mother, back toward the lobby to find her twin.

Carrie breathed out a long-suffering mother sigh. "You look wonderful, Gina. It would be fun to go to a ball. I feel like I haven't had a reason to dress up in ages."

"Thanks, Car." Gina twisted her fingers, watching her friend. "Listen, do you mind if I ask you something? I've been thinking about my life and what I can balance lately. And how Ben fits into it." She took a step closer to Carrie, who was just a few years older than Gina, but wore concern and responsibility like a second skin. "You were married, you had kids, the house, the husband. A safe, predictable life. Do you ever regret any of that? Do you ever wish you'd have done things differently?"

"I'm a parent. I question myself every day." The smile that curved Carrie's face was sad. "But if I could go back? I wish I'd married for love, instead of practicality." She lifted her shoulders, resigned. "I wish I'd taken the time to live a little more and have some fun. But I have a good life, divorce and all. I shouldn't complain."

"Thanks." Gina slipped her arms around her friend, appreciating her honesty, but not any surer of herself than before.

Lena popped her head in. "He's here!"

Gina moved into the lobby, her mouth going dry and heart flip-flopping, much the way it had when Ben had first surprised her after his deployment. His dress blues never failed to impress.

"My lady." He held out his arm. "May I escort you to the Marine Corps Birthday ball?"

"Careful, being so perfect." She waved her hands in front of her eyes and blinked away rising emotion. "You'll make me ruin my face."

Ben hooked her hand to his arm. "Not possible."

Glowing from the inside out with his quiet confidence, Gina shoved her concerns into the corners of her mind and nearly floated out of the hotel.

Ben

THE LAST SIX weeks had been amazing. Quiet dinners at her apartment, grocery shopping together on Saturday mornings, evenings watching her work her event magic at the hotel, nights wrapped around each other in her bed. It was fun and sexy and so damn normal, he wanted it—wanted her—forever. And though Ben had never been a betting man—he was always the guy in the corner reading a book while the rest of the fire team played poker —his time east with Gina had been so good, so solid, he'd gambled.

The small ring box in his pocket didn't have to come out tonight. It could wait. He figured he would know when the time was right, when Gina let the last of her reservations go. Maybe it would be tonight, maybe not. He'd prepared himself for either outcome.

She was beautiful, a sparkling blond princess on his arm who he led proudly into the ballroom, hosted by the unit he'd be transferring into if he wanted to be closer to Gina. They got drinks and found their table where two other couples were seated. Ben made the required small talk with the other Marines at the table but mostly indulged himself in watching Gina do her professional chit-chat with the wives. Occasionally he'd run a hand over the ring box in his pocket, trying to quiet the urge to drop to his knee right there by the table.

After several speeches, Gina turned to the woman to her right, Sue. "When does the dancing start?" Gina squeezed Ben's hand where she held it under the table. "I made this guy promise he'd dance with me."

Sue laughed. "This must be your first ball. The speeches are over so any minute now the party will really start. This is my... let's see. Sixteenth ball, probably? Harrison and I got married right out of high school and we've only missed it when he was overseas."

"Wow." Ben watched curiosity grow on Gina's face and she leaned in closer. "Over fifteen years as a military spouse. How has that been? Have you had to move at all?"

Apprehension skittered across his skin at her question, and he resisted the urge to squeeze her hand.

"Honey, I am a professional mover." Sue laughed again, glancing with affection across the table to where her husband engaged in deep conversation with another officer. "We've moved seven times. I had our youngest when he was in Afghanistan." She laughed again when she said it, evidently at ease with their lifestyle, while Gina's face registered horror. "You can't rely on a schedule with a military spouse. Instead, you get good at adapting. Good at making friends. And being independent."

"I'm good at being independent." Gina's voice was paper-thin, shell-shocked. Ben put his free hand on the back of her neck to soothe, hoping he could avoid the train wreck building behind her eyes. "But that's a lot. How do you build anything of your own that way? And the deployments, not knowing…how do you get through them?"

Sue's eyes softened and she reached out, laying a gentle hand on Gina's arm. "You just do. You have faith in him"—she nodded toward Ben—"and in yourself. That's all you can do."

Nodding, Gina sat back, pulling her hand from Ben's grasp to rub her arms as if cold.

Ben silently swore. This wasn't supposed to be how things went. When the DJ started pumping music, it seemed like a lifeline.

"Why don't we dance, Snowflake?" He tipped her chin to look into her troubled sea-green eyes. "What do you say?"

She nodded, and he led her to join the other couples swaying to the remake of a 1980s classic. When he wrapped his arms around her, Ben smiled, feeling more confident. "This has got to be the worst version of "Take My Breath Away" I've ever heard."

A small smile touched Gina's lips and her chilly fingers fluttered at the edge of his neck. "It is pretty bad."

"You'd do a much better job. Maybe you should go grab the mic and turn this into karaoke."

"You really think I would do that?" Her brows pinched with insult.

"Well, maybe not here." He didn't understand why she seemed upset. "But a different party, or at a bar? Sure. That's classic Gina."

"What if you tire of the real me? What if I embarrass you, or you get sick of waiting for me? You don't even have to decide to leave me. The military will do it for you."

Ben blinked down at her, trying to catch up with her logic. "I've only ever known the real you. That's who I fell in love with. I won't get tired of you. It's possible I get sent away, but if it's up to me, I'll always choose to be with you."

"I'm afraid you're going to figure out that I'm this fraud." Gina blinked watery eyes. "And I'm going to be left high and dry all over again. I know I've grown up a lot, and I'm not the crazy kid I used to be. And you're not Dustin. But I'm still me. Why would you be any different? Why would things between us work? I want a guarantee."

"Gina, I can't guarantee anything." Ben pressed his forehead to hers, aching for her to understand. "I can promise that I bone-deep love you and will support you in your work or your crafts or, hell, if you wanted to go back into theater. But there are no guarantees in life." He'd seen that for himself.

She allowed herself to be pulled against him, settling in for several beats until her hand dropped, brushed over his pocket. Hovering for a moment over the lump, Gina dipped her fingers inside. She touched the jeweler's box, then yanked away as if stung.

"What's in your pocket?"

"Hope." He was sick of apologizing for wanting the

traditional commitment, for wanting it all. For wanting to grab what was good in life and never let go.

"A ring, Ben?" She took a half step away, panic in her eyes.

"Relax. I'm not forcing you into anything."

"I told you. I need to be independent."

"You are. That's one of your best qualities. A ring won't change that." Ben stepped in close again, even as she went stiff under his hands. Fear lodged inside him alongside frustration. "But there's a fine line between independent and alone, Snowflake."

"Maybe alone is safer. I love you too but I told you I wasn't sure if I was ready for a relationship. If something happens to you and I'm that invested…if you leave again…I don't know if I can take it."

"You aren't ready for a relationship?" Ben's laugh was mirthless, her resistance a needle to a deepening wound. They were drawing looks from the others on the dance floor now, but he hurt too much to care. "Too late, sweet cheeks, you're in one. What do you think this is?"

"Don't you try to pen me in, you musclebound cowboy soldier," Gina slapped back. "If you're so patient and willing to support me, why is marriage always your answer?"

Fuming, Ben stepped in so they were nose to nose. "I'm no soldier, I'm a goddamn Marine. A shit cowboy, mediocre son. But damn good Marine. I wasn't looking for a curly-haired screwball with more professional motivation than a bunch of Ivy Leaguers, but we got stuck together and it's the best damn thing that ever happened to me."

She backed up again, jaw clenched, and the air between them went from fire to freezing.

"Snowflake, I've been patient." He was so fucking tired of being patient. Life waited for nobody and what they had was solid. "We're good together, you see it as well as I do. I've played your game the way you wanted, on your timeline. But I'm done getting only bits and pieces while we're miles apart. We could be together. We could have everything."

She blinked hard, shaking her head and the pain of failure was like a mortar round going off in his chest.

"That's what I want. Everything." Ben couldn't keep the anger out of his voice anymore. He'd stripped himself bare for her and she still couldn't see the truth. "You've trapped yourself in a tower, princess. But I didn't build it. You did."

"You're right. I did." Gina straightened, all icy pride even as her chin quivered. If he wasn't so broken, he'd have admired it. "And that's where I'm going to stay."

She turned on her heel, weaving through the crowd of dancers, and out the door.

Ben watched as she disappeared, then looked down at his chest, numbly surprised he wasn't bleeding out. Because that was what it felt like.

THE CHRISTMAS THEY SORTED IT OUT (AGAIN)

BEN

"Can I help with something?"

Ben's dad snorted. "Naw. I've a cow with a bad foot I gotta doctor. Brian will help me. Why don't you go service the skid steer?" He added with a wink, "We don't need any cattle disasters."

He went out the door in a cloud of cold air, Brian trailing behind.

Ben's mother rolled her eyes. "Don't you mind him. Tractors can wait. Stay here and keep me company while I plug in these numbers." She stabbed at the office laptop, looking over lines of cattle records, her long dark auburn hair in a braid down her back.

He sat down on the small wooden stool next to her with a flop. It was a good thing the Marines taught him how to embrace misery. Ben had thought that by now, weeks since Gina had cut him off, that the ache in his chest would have eased, but it remained. And watching his parents together somehow made it worse. "Mom, how did you know you wanted to be with dad? You two are so perfect together."

"Perfect? Hon, there's nothing perfect about the way your father and I are together. I didn't want to be a rancher's housewife. And I'm not. We're a couple of puzzle pieces that fit, but there are gaps, overlaps, and it takes work to make things seamless."

She squinted at the screen, and Ben handed her the reading glasses she'd left hooked to her flannel shirt pocket.

Bonnie smiled and slipped them on. "I wanted a partner, an equal place in the business, and I expected him to be equal in the home. Not a man providing everything while I raised the children. It took some tough conversations to get that squared away, but I stuck to my guns on what was important to me, and he did on what was important to him, and we met near the middle."

She looked at him over her glasses. "I didn't want to be my mother, bless her. And we've fought our way through it sometimes. But he's my best friend and my partner. We're not perfect together, but we're right. Both of us give a little for the other."

Ben steepled his fingers, liking his mother's answer. Liking more the way it shifted something inside him slightly, making room where he'd been reluctant to give up space. He could see now, after weeks of radio silence, that he'd pushed Gina too hard. And she'd been waiting for a reason to run.

"Now, I want to talk about you. How much longer am I going to have to worry about my baby going to war?"

"Not for a while with this new MOS. And after…I don't think I'm coming back home, Mom. Not for good."

"I know. This was never your natural place." She squeezed his hand. "I don't mean you're not welcome. We love you and the door is always open, but it isn't where you belong."

Ben squeezed back. "No. I don't fit here with you guys. For a while I was thinking of transferring to the East Coast. Thought I'd found my place with a person, with Gina." But he'd killed that with the all-or-nothing ultimatum, an action he regretted, even though he knew it might have happened eventually. She'd been right to question his patience. "The fitness trainer thing is pretty good so far. I can see doing that when I'm out."

"You'll figure it out. Just be honest with yourself." She looked over her glasses at him again. "And flexible with Gina. White picket-fence-happy looks different for everyone."

Brian came back in the door, stomping snow off his boots, and Ben stood.

"No matter what, we're behind you." Bonnie snapped the laptop shut. "Now it's time to go get cleaned up. We have to get to the Smith Christmas party."

"Aww, Ma, do we have to?" Brian whined; ten years old all over again.

Ben couldn't resist a small smile, wondered what the odds were that Gina was getting dragged to the party with a similar lack of excitement.

"Yes." Her eyes glinted, looking squarely at Ben. "It's going to be a good one."

Gina

"What are you doing? Why aren't you ready for the party?"

"I'm not going." Pleasantly miserable, Gina unwrapped another chocolate kiss and stuffed it in her mouth, not bothering to look at her sister. "Now move. You're blocking my view and the prince is about to take off his cravat."

"There are a hundred people heading up Mom and Dad's driveway, and you're still in your sweats." Natalie kicked an empty popcorn bag. "This is worse than I thought."

"Huh?" Gina blinked, realizing her sister was still there. She was in a junk food coma, celebrating the holidays and her recent promotion to Director of Events for the Davidson Hotel chain by attempting to give herself diabetes. The last thing she wanted to do in the remaining two days of her Christmas visit with her family was the damn party. All the people. The Richardsons.

Natalie clicked the television off. "Look, when I pushed you and Ben together, I didn't think it would get this complicated. I should have realized. You both are stubborn as mules."

Gina had confided the whole sordid tale over a couple of bottles of wine earlier in the visit, and now regretted it. Misery was a pretty good bedfellow if you really committed to it, she thought. And since it had been her constant companion since she'd had her meltdown at the ball, they'd gotten pretty familiar.

"On your feet." Nat grabbed Gina's hands and hauled her up.

"Leave me be. I haven't melted into the couch yet."

"Shut up. Do you love Ben?"

Gina blew out a breath. That was easy. "Yes."

"Does he love you?"

"He said he did. And he's only ever been honest." Her heart squeezed painfully.

"The ass who left you in debt, did he love you?"

Gina gave her a flat stare. *Obviously Not.*

"Did you do something impulsive to piss Ben off?"

"Maybe." She knew she'd overreacted at the ball, but then, he'd been a domineering jerk. And it seemed like if they were meant to be, then it should be easy. Except things didn't feel any easier now that they were apart. They felt hollow and depressing.

"Did he do something pushy to piss you off?"

"Yes."

Natalie yanked the ties on Gina's sweatshirt, bringing home her point.

"Are you happier now without Ben, or were you happier with him?"

Gina looked down at herself. She'd been getting through work, going through the motions, keeping clients happy, her boss happy. But she wasn't happy.

It can't possibly be that simple. Can it?

"With him."

"Excellent. What a bright student you are." Natalie clapped her hands together. "The man's not a coat rack. Don't let him go because you can't figure out how to make him fit in a particular box. And for that matter, stop trying to put yourself in one. Now, get your stinky rear end in the shower and get down to this party. I'm getting you and Ben under the mistletoe tonight if it kills me."

"But…" Gina swallowed down the hope that crept up her chest. "What if he rejects me?"

Nat reached out, squeezed her arm. "At least you went down swinging."

"I'm scared. What if…what if marriage makes us like Mom and Dad?" She needed more reassurance. She'd always thought she was so tough and brave. Love exposed your sensitive underbelly. "Are you happy?"

"Babe, I'm happy because I married the best man for me. I am not our mother, and neither are you. Ben isn't Dad." She pulled Gina in for a quick hug. "They're part of your heritage, not your destiny." Nat let go and pushed Gina back toward the bathroom. "Come on, now. Time to make a romantic fool of yourself."

"Do I have to?

"Do you want him?"

Like air to breathe.

"Nat?" Her sister paused in the doorway and looked back. "Thanks for saying no when he proposed."

Natalie grinned. "Anytime, sis."

A quick shower and fight with the hair dryer later, Gina stood in her bedroom staring at her phone. For almost two years, the device had been her primary connection to Ben. The death of that connection left a more acute hole in her life than she ever could have imagined.

Months before, they'd enabled location sharing. She watched Ben's, the little blue location bubble hovering on her own. He was in the house right now. Within reach, if she had the guts to make a move.

Gina closed her eyes. If he was sent away, could she survive? Would they?

Yes, damnit. The warm glow of confidence grew as she considered. If she was as independent as she claimed to be, they could do this. It was time for her to stop doubting herself long enough to give them a chance. They both deserved it.

Tossing the phone to the coffee table, she took off down the hall and into the swarm of partygoers before she could come up with more excuses.

"Hey, Ginny! Look at you—"

"Not now, Jenkin." She breezed by him. Mrs. LaBree shuffled into her path and she barely slowed down, offering a polite "Merry Christmas" as she made her way into the living room.

This was a moment she'd remember forever and she needed it to start right now.

Gina blew out a steadying breath while "Jingle Bells" played over the speakers, just audible over the chatter of the party. People packed the room. But through them all, there was Ben, back under the Santa cows, frown in place.

You've got this, Snowflake. Make him proud.

She took a moment to identify the best vantage point to make a scene. The potential for embarrassment was absolute. But just seeing him had her heart throbbing with a hopeful beat, and for the first time in years she didn't care one iota what anyone in the room thought of her. She cared only about Ben.

Maneuvering through the crowded room, Gina found her way to the center, next to the couch. Ben's dark forest green eyes locked with hers, eyes she used to think were mysterious. Now they were as familiar to her as her own. The noise of the room fell away, and for a long heartbeat, it was just the two of them. And she knew what to do.

The voices came crashing back as Gina kicked off her heels, using the shoulder of the nearest person to climb on top of the side table, knocking a full candy dish onto the couch in the process. Never breaking eye contact with Ben.

"Excuse me." Her voice wobbled for only a moment, then came back full and strong. "Hey! I have something I have to say."

"Are you going to sing for us, Ginny?" Brian called out. At the sharp look from his brother, he added, "What? She's a great singer."

"Gina, what on earth? Get down from there." Her mother attempted to cut through the milling guests, who had gone quiet with the treat of a spectacle.

"Truth." She took a steadying breath, ignoring her mother, and looked back across the room again to find Ben. "I once promised you no scenes. Well, I lied."

The onlookers cackled.

"Truth. I trust you. I love you. And I want to be with you. To fight and laugh and make a home. And—" Her voice threatened to break but she bore down. "Maybe that means we won't always be able to be together, physically. In the same place. But I still want it. I want to be there to wake you from your nightmares and to make love with you. Truth. I believe we can make it, just as we are, as broken and imperfect as we are. Right now."

She blinked away the tears that threatened to fall. "And I...I dare you to marry me, Ben Richardson, if you'll still have me."

All eyes turned to gauge Ben's reaction, a murmur of snickers moving through the room like a wave as he stood, face impassive. A choking breath got caught in Gina's chest, all hope crashing away, until his mouth finally quirked in a smile. "I will."

Stunned silence followed the statement, even as he carved his way through the crowd to stand below her.

Tears streamed down Gina's face, but she didn't bother wiping them away, too relieved to care how she looked or what anyone thought. "I love you so much, Ben."

"I know. I love you too. Jump on down here, Snowflake." Ben reached up, gripped her waist. "I'm here to catch you."

Their lips met in a smile, arms wrapping each other in the most precious gift, to the raucous cheers and applause of the crowd.

"I'm sorry I pushed you too hard, too fast." Ben's lips brushed her ear, and she shivered, his warmth filling all the cold, empty places inside her. "We're both a couple of stubborn fools."

"I'm sorry I made a spectacle of you with all of this." Gina's fingers gripped each other around his neck, unwilling to let go.

Someone started singing "All I Want for Christmas is You," and the rest of the room joined in, and Gina choked on a laugh full of happy relief. Maybe her hometown wasn't quite as awful as she liked to think.

"At least we made them wait a few years for this show." He brushed his lips across both her cheeks. "And I like the way this one ended a lot better."

EPILOGUE

GINA

"Are you ready for this?" Gina leaned on the door, tilting her ear to hear Ben's response through the thick metal.

"Snowflake, I've been ready for this since I walked into this hotel and saw you again after Afghanistan."

Love warmed her from the inside out and she smiled, looking down at the sparkling engagement ring and deep red wedding day manicure. She'd never forget that moment either, or the sense of completeness his presence had offered.

"Have you heard from Ryan or Greer yet? They should be here by now." She should have known better than to have a wedding so close to Christmas. A monster snowstorm had wreaked havoc with the flights, and last she'd heard, the two were stuck somewhere in the Midwest, with the wedding only a few hours away.

"They'll do their best. But even if they don't, it's not the end of the world. You're here. My parents and Brian. That's what matters." She heard him huff out a dark laugh. "Hell, I've got Hodges in here drinking half the bar. I've done more with less."

Carrie scurried up the hall and Gina caught her eye, speaking with deliberate confidence through the door. "They'll be here." Ben would put on a brave face, but having Ryan and Greer standing with him at the wedding meant more to him than he'd ever admit.

He'd uprooted his life so they could be together, transferring units so she could stay at Davidson. And if she could give him anything in the world, it was the same sense of peace that he gave her. Snagging Carrie's hand, she stood and turned to the door again. "I've got to go now and get beautiful for you."

"You don't have to get beautiful. You are beautiful."

God, she loved him. He said it so simply, so honestly.

"Thank you. I love you. I'll see you soon. You can finally make an honest woman out of me."

As intended, the last comment had Ben grumbling and laughing at the same time. "Finally, my ass. Like I was the one resistant to marriage…"

"What are you doing here?" Carrie caught Gina's elbow and not-so-subtly drove her down the hall and into the elevator, toward the bridal suite. "You're supposed to start makeup in"—she glanced at her phone, pinging with alerts—"five minutes."

Carrie had taken on much of Gina's typical role within the hotel for the event, on top of her regular duties.

"I know, I know. I'm not trying to mess up the timetable. I just had to check in with Ben." She turned, took her friend by the arms so she could look into her eyes. "Carrie, I need you."

Carrie's brow creased with concern. "Sure. Anything."

"You've got to find Ryan and Greer. Ben's groomsmen. This is so important to him. He's playing it cool, but it matters that they're here." She felt bad putting the added stress on Carrie's shoulders, but she was the most dogged, detail-oriented person Gina had ever known, and if anyone could find a couple of missing Marines, it was Carrie. "I'm sure they're trying, but could you track them down?"

"I'm on it." Carrie offered a determined smile as she opened the door to the bridal suite, where Andrea, Nat, and Gina's mother and grandmother were already getting ready. "Now go, it's makeup time."

As directed, Gina settled in for the stylist. Twenty minutes later her phone chirped.

> Carrie 3:00 PM: Their flight is on the ground in Philly.

> Carrie 3:30: I'll have the front desk keep an eye out.

> Carrie 4:25: Don't worry. Just going to check with the front desk again.

> Carrie 4:43: They're here and unbelievably hot. Why didn't you warn me?

Doing her best not to ruin the stylists' work, Gina laughed and blinked back tears of relief at the same time, mentally high-fiving herself for trusting Carrie.

Hours later, with the pressure of the ceremony completed, Gina and Ben swayed slowly on the dance floor of their reception.

With her face tucked under his chin, Ben's fingers steadily stroking the exposed flesh along her back. "I hear you put Carrie on the boys' trail this afternoon. Thanks."

"I am not above using my stellar professional skills and contacts for personal gain." Gina kissed his jaw, lingering on the spot just above the collar of his dress blues. She couldn't wait to get him out of his clothes…but maybe she could get him to do a little private dance later. The kind that involved removing the uniform very slowly. "It was peace of mind for both of us."

As if he could read her thoughts, Ben growled and captured her mouth with his own. When they came up for air, Gina did a double take over his shoulder.

"Speaking of Carrie." She gestured to where Ryan and her friend embraced in a dance, gazes locked as if the rest of the world didn't exist. "That could be a problem."

"I don't know. We figured it out." A smile curved Ben's mouth, and he glanced at the other couple, then back at his bride for a long beat. "She'd be good for him."

"He'd be good for her." Gina quirked a brow. "But. There are a lot of miles between them."

"It's a good thing they have friends like us, then." Ben brought her knuckles to his lips, pressing a kiss to them tenderly. "To help them figure out how to manage it. Together."

His smile reached his rich green eyes and Gina's did too, even as they spilled over with the overpowering joy. "Every mile."

WANT Gina and Ben's spicy bonus scene? Sign up for my newsletter at jaimepbradley.com for exclusive access to bonus content, and for a chance to download my next new release for free!

Read on for a sample of Ryan and Carrie's story, *3000 Reasons to Stay*, or buy it now HERE.

3000 REASONS TO STAY

CHAPTER 1: HUSTLE

Carrie Waller knew if she didn't start saying no, there was a very real chance her closest relationship would be with her phone notifications.

No to the last-minute project requests from her boss. No to her ex-husband when he wanted her to run interference with the other hotel staff or cover an open shift on the front desk. And no to the volunteer requests from her daughters' school and sports teams—even though admitting she didn't have time for something related to the girls brought on an epic case of mom guilt.

And she would. Tomorrow. Right after she made today perfect for her best friend, Gina.

Ding. Pick up dry cleaning, fifteen minutes ago.

Ding. Update checklist and review with Gina's wedding planner, ten minutes.

Ding. Get dessert to PTA holiday fundraiser, one hour.

Carrie skimmed the barrage of alerts and took a steadying breath. Don't kill the messenger, she thought just as a new text message from her boss blinked on the screen. Even if it would be satisfying to crunch the damn thing under the heel of her chunky snow boots. It might even give her a few minutes peace.

Just imagining violence against the electronic device momentarily eased the pressure throbbing behind her eyes as she kicked the boots off and stepped into her black slides.

"You're not wearing that, are you?"

Ignoring her sister Andrea's question—and the automatic resentment that bloomed—Carrie hung her reliable little black dress swathed in dry cleaner's plastic on the back of her office door and continued to read the latest request from her boss—and former mother-in-law—this time to create and send a satisfaction survey for all the guests at Gina's wedding.

The wedding of her close friend and coworker. Taking place in just over four hours. Perfect. One more thing to do.

Carrie gritted her teeth and logged into her computer with forceful jabs before glancing at Andrea, who had flopped down in the opposite chair and propped her feet next to the miniature vintage ceramic Christmas tree glowing on the corner of the desk. Andrea's oak-brown hair had been expertly curled in relaxed waves by the bridal stylist, half pulled back and pinned with pearl beads, just as Gina had wanted for her bridesmaids.

"Your hair looks great." Pride and excitement eased some of the anxiety wrapping its arms around Carrie's shoulders as she imagined the finished product—dark blue dresses, perfect makeup, her sister's beauty alongside Gina's glowing happiness. Then reality squeezed back in. "You didn't leave Gina's mother alone with her, did you?"

"Relax. Her mom and Grandma are busy having their makeup done, and I took Gina's phone like you wanted." Andrea held up the device next to her own as proof, then paused to examine her shimmering pearl manicure. "They can't harass her for at least twenty minutes. I'm just down here for a delivery. Gina wanted cheesy bread."

Carrie whooshed out a relieved breath. "Thank you."

A message from the front desk pinged. The floral arrangements had arrived, and the setup team was putting them out. Carrie automatically updated the e-checklist she shared with the wedding planner.

She still needed to check on setup status of the ballroom, pray to the weather gods that the snow tapered off enough for the ceremony to be held in the courtyard like Gina wanted, arrange the PTA dessert delivery, and send her boss the satisfaction survey. Not to mention determine if the last two groomsmen—whose flights had been impacted by the weather—had finally arrived.

Carrie pressed through the familiar sense of overwhelm by reviewing her checklist, enjoying the half-second thrill of striking off the completed tasks.

When she'd offered to act as coordinator for the event being held in Davidson Hotel's downtown Wilmington, Delaware, location, it felt like the least she could do for her close friend and coworker. Work was a gift she knew how to give. But the added pressures of the day threatened to topple the carefully constructed Jenga tower that was her sanity.

"Seriously though, that dress has been done to death."

"We're back to this?" Weary of always defending her practical choices, Carrie couldn't stop irritation from lacing the words. She pushed back from her seat to dig through her purse for Tic Tacs.

Andrea recrossed her ankles on the desk, appearing effortlessly sexy and carefree as usual. "I'm just saying, you're single. There are going to be a ton of single Marines there tonight, dancing, drinking, and having fun." She looked up from the phone screens in her hand to assess her big sister with a raised brow. "You do remember what fun is, right?"

Ding. Review with wedding planner, two minutes.

Ding. Status update on wedding party, thirty minutes.

Carrie glanced at the reminders, continuing to paw through the gigantic mom purse, knowing she sounded defensive. "I have fun." She paused her search to stab at the screen of her phone to text a check-in with the wedding planner. Watching her daughters play soccer was fun, as were their movie sessions when she came off a late shift. And work could be. Sometimes. Her gaze drifted to the photo of Lena and Viv on her desk, grinning at their eighth-grade graduation that past spring. "What does fun have to do with my dress?"

"You should look hot, and it's not." Andrea pointed a finger at her. "Honestly, when was the last time you got laid?"

Carrie shook her head, exasperation overflowing. By choice, Andrea was partnerless, childless, didn't own a car or a home. She wasn't weighed down by any obligations, besides her shifts as a traveling intensive care nurse and doing what pleased her.

Carrie loved her sister. But Andrea didn't get it.

"I have two kids, live with my mother, and work for my ex-husband and his parents. I might as well have I'VE GOT BAGGAGE tattooed on my forehead. Sex is just a memory." She lifted her chin, reining in the emotions. "I love Gina, and I want her day with Ben to be perfect, but it is essentially a work event for me. It doesn't matter if I have fun."

The epic failure that was her personal life didn't need to be dealt with today. That was a problem for tomorrow. She had other obligations. The hollow in her chest she felt at the end of the day wasn't loneliness. It was exhaustion.

"Do you realize all the moving parts for an event like this? I'm going to be busy the whole time." She gave up on the black hole that was her purse and tossed it aside to dive into the desk drawer for her emergency stash of mints. "It doesn't matter how I look. It's not like I'm going to meet my true love tonight or have a sexy encounter at my place of work. What matters is that it goes off without a hitch."

"Ah, yes. I almost forgot. If it's not in your phone calendar or something the girls or your bosses want, then it doesn't exist." Andrea shook her head in disdain. "You're one wool sweater away from putting your lady bits in mothballs. And I don't like it, Car, not one bit. You're thirty-four. Way too young for mothballs."

Carrie shook several Tic Tacs into her hand and tossed them in her mouth, relishing the familiar burn of mint. At twenty-six,

Andrea felt she was worldly enough to criticize despite the years between them. Then again, Andrea had been speaking her mind since the day she'd learned to talk. Usually it was one of Carrie's favorite attributes.

She shoved the sense of defeat beneath the need to move on with her day. The sooner she got Andrea to the point, the sooner she could get the next to-do done. "Dre, why do you care?"

"Maybe with Gina getting married and the holidays and all, I'm feeling sentimental."

Carrie gave her sister a blank stare.

Andrea grinned. "That didn't sound believable to me either. Look, I don't know. You're running around doing everything for everyone, and I just think this is a great opportunity to give them all the finger."

Aah. There it was. Andrea had never understood her choice to continue working with Sam and his parents since the divorce. Carrie's heart squeezed painfully with emotion. Leave it to her bighearted, potty-mouthed, free-bird sister to show love with a curse. A wobbly laugh escaped. "That's what this is really about. You want me to quit."

Ding. Verify all bridal/groomsmen prep progress, ninety minutes.

Ding. Sit in on Food and Beverage team meeting, ten minutes.

Ding. Schedule McCabe job interview, one day ago.

Carrie stared at the reminder that had been repeating hourly since the day before when the interview offer had arrived. After a particularly frustrating week at Davidson a month earlier, a wine-fueled job search had resulted in her applying for the assistant manager role with McCabe Hotels. The position at the well-regarded employer was one that could not only be a step up in her career but also wouldn't require a move.

Because Sam would forever be tied to Davidson Hotels, and Helena and Vivian were tied to their father. And, therefore, so was she. No matter how ready she was for escape.

But it wasn't a task for today, if ever. She hit Ignore yet again, acid churning in her stomach, and stood.

"Thank you. I appreciate the thought, but I'm not giving anyone the finger. It's too late for a new dress, but if it'll make you feel better, I'll let you do my makeup." She'd never been any good at the smoky eye, and Andrea was a pro. "I want to check on Gina and I have to get to a meeting, then assess setup."

"I think I have something," Andrea mumbled, distracted by the two phones lighting up in her lap. "It didn't fit me, but your tits are smaller."

Suppressing a smile, Carrie headed toward the door.

As her hand hit the knob, an alert announcing a change to Viv and Lena's soccer practice that day had her stifling a groan. They were already cutting it close, finishing practice in time to dress for the wedding. Carrie closed her eyes against the sense of drowning. No matter how she mentally rearranged the rest of her afternoon, there were too many things going on to get them to the field house and back home to get ready.

She dialed Sam. Her ex's voice came on the line, Saturday sleepy and easygoing, and she tried not to let her anxiety leak through.

"The girls' soccer practice time got changed. Can you pick them up? I'm tied up here."

"Sure. I've got nothing until the wedding."

Envy prickled her spine, but her voice stayed polite. "Thanks. Actually, if you're not busy, the PTA is doing another cakewalk fundraiser this afternoon at the holiday bazaar. We're going to miss it, obviously, but I told them I would bring in a dessert. I haven't had a chance to drop one off. Since you'll be at the school, could you swing by the store and bring something? I've got a lot going on here."

"The PTA's really your thing."

"Yes, but it's for *our* children's school." Carrie's eye twitched, and she pressed a finger to it. "You know what? Never mind. I'll take care of it."

Seemingly oblivious to her frustration, Sam mumbled agreement. "By the way, Wednesday afternoon I need you at the department heads meeting."

The anxiety arms around her shoulders squeezed tighter, and she fought to breathe normally. "I have that afternoon off. For a doctor's appointment." Her annual GYN exam, not that it was any of his business. "It's been scheduled for months."

She could practically hear him shrugging in apology. "Mom got the sales team from PROdux to commit, and we need you to be there."

Being needed was nice, and maybe being handed extra work a kind of flattery of its own, but at the moment it felt like a backhanded insult. Like the time her former mother-in-law had given her Spanx for her birthday after the twins were born. *Umm, thanks?*

It was all Carrie could do not to reach through the phone and shake Sam until his teeth rattled. Imagining it made her feel a little better actually, and she let out a slow breath. Get through today, that was the goal, then she would worry about next week.

"I'll see what I can do."

Call ended, Carrie slumped against the door. The metal cooled the knots in her back while panic laced the edges of her vision. She was running late, and she didn't have time for a meltdown. Gina deserved a perfect wedding day, and Carrie was going to make it all happen even if it killed her. She just had to figure out how.

3000 REASONS TO STAY

CHAPTER 2: EMBRACE THE SUCK

This wasn't how today was supposed to go.

Running down the slush-filled shoulder of Interstate 95 in downtown Wilmington, past the bumper-to-bumper stopped traffic, dress blues uniform slung over his back with barely more than an hour before his best friend's wedding.

But that was exactly what Marine Gunnery Sergeant Ryan Duran and Staff Sergeant Greer DeAngelo were doing. Getting there was a task with an achievable goal, one Ryan was happy to focus on. Rather than on how the friendship would change with Ben's marriage and move. Rather than on how getting there might be the only thing in his life right now that was straightforward.

"This blows. We should be a couple drinks in with Ben right now." Greer's stride matched Ryan's as they continued down the highway away from their stranded Uber. "I wanted to have time to scope out the bridesmaid situation before all the scheduled shit."

Thankful he'd looked at the address of the hotel where the wedding was taking place before his phone had died, Ryan checked his watch and picked up speed. "If we maintain this pace, we'll be there in under ten minutes."

"Hell, Gunny. This was supposed to be my off day." But

Greer's smile flashed white against tanned olive skin as he equaled the pace, the Marine instinct to dominate any challenge, no matter how shitty or dumb, on full display.

"You got a better idea? We're not letting Ben do this thing without backup." Ryan glanced at the steel gray sky; the fat wet flakes of snow that had caused chaos on the highway finally had ended. After nineteen years in the military, he knew how to hump miles in miserable conditions and learn to like it, to embrace the suck. And this royally sucked. Flying commercial in December was always perilous, but nothing would keep them from the wedding. Not even two canceled flights and multiple delays.

Ryan's feet hit the pavement steadily, winter wind slapping his cheeks as he looked ahead at the exit marker for Fourth Street and felt a modicum of relief.

He and Ben had joined the fleet at the same time and had chewed a lot of ground together. Ben, his second in command as a Marine Force Fitness Instructor for the last couple years and his friend for more than a decade, had just transferred units from San Diego to be with Gina in Wilmington. Ryan promised Ben that he and Greer would be there to stand with him, and it was going to happen, even if their frozen corpses had to be propped beside the altar.

Ryan flexed his cold-stiff fingers around the hanger and forced himself to focus on the steady pounding in his chest as they turned off the exit ramp, ignoring the twinge of jealousy at the thought of his friend moving on with his life, settling down. Planning a different future, outside the Corps. Something he should do himself.

"I can't believe Richardson's really getting married." Between the puffs of breath, the disdain in Greer's voice was unmistakable. "And ditching Southern California for this."

He gestured to the white-dusted trees twinkling with Christmas lights alongside grubby piles of half-frozen snow.

"For the woman, dumbass. Hell, Gina's kept him waiting for how many years now? He'd agree to live in Siberia if that's what she wanted." Ryan shook his head, not entirely understanding but unable to resist a smile at the thought of the little spitfire his friend had fallen for. And had the patience to lock down, even if it'd taken longer than Ben wanted. "Have you seen his face lately whenever he sees a text from her? He's so damn nervous she'll change her mind, he looks like he's about to have a heart attack."

Greer looked longingly at a pizza shop as they ran by. "I have too much fun sampling all the flavors of women. Committing to one taste would ruin the total experience."

Ryan glanced at Greer before dodging an icy puddle. "Food metaphors?"

"What? It's been hours since the airplane cookies." They split around a couple arm-in-arm in the middle of the sidewalk. "Think you'll ever settle down, Gunny? Those pretty boy looks of yours won't last forever."

"Fuck off." Ryan only resisted stiff arming Greer into a snowbank because it would slow them down. End up on a couple Marine recruitment billboards and chosen to lead an online video Marine fitness series...he'd never live it down. Even if he'd collected too many scars over the years to be considered the pretty boy of his youth.

"I don't know." That seemed to be the answer to everything lately, and it ate at him. "For the right person, maybe." For someone who would stick by him, an elusive ghost of a person he'd been thinking of more and more. "Ben got a good one with Gina. I'm just impressed they did the long-distance thing that long and made it to the other side. That shit's hard." He knew firsthand how easily those relationships crashed and burned.

Greer grunted agreement as they turned the corner onto North Shipley and the green and gold Davidson Hotel awning came into view. The heat of the lobby smacked Ryan in the face as they stepped through the revolving doors, and he took a moment to take stock, satisfied with the steady beat of his heart, the way his muscles had warmed and performed under less-than-ideal conditions. His body was his business, his biggest asset. He paid attention to it because at thirty-seven, he was beginning to feel every fiber more acutely.

At the moment, that being half frozen, in sopping wet sneakers and a shirt and light jacket soaked through from sweat and snow. Now to find Ben, a hot shower, and get the real show on the road. One last mission together.

While Greer bought out the sandwich stock in the small lobby café, Ryan checked them in. As soon as he had their room keys in hand, they took off, turning the corner for the bank of elevators at a jog. And a nose smashed into his chest.

Ryan looked down at the top of a woman's head wrapped in a white towel, her hot breath pressing through the cold fabric of his shirt. She wobbled a moment, and he reached out to steady her awkwardly, arms draped in both his and Greer's uniform bags. "Whoa, you all right?"

She stepped back quickly, crimson rushing a face recently washed clean. Warm brown eyes stared forward at his chest, then up his neck, before finally climbing all the way to his face, as if she wasn't sure exactly what she was looking at.

"I'm so sorry..." She swallowed hard. "I was texting and walking." A phone poked out from the long sleeve of the robe. An outfit, he noticed, paired with gray snow boots. "Dangerous combination."

"We're good." He tried to smile, but his face was stiff, as if he still stood out in the cold. "Don't worry about it."

She looked again at both of them, eyes lingering on the military green garment bags and their undoubtedly bedraggled appearance. And then they absolutely lit, bouncing back to Ryan's face, sending a shot of warmth to the depths of his chest, momentarily stealing his power of speech. "You're the groomsmen!"

Greer swallowed a massive bite of turkey sandwich. "For Ben and Gina's wedding, yeah." He revealed his killer dimples. "Better late than never, am I right?"

"Oh, thank god." She looked between them. "Stay, right here."

And she took off, clomping around the corner toward the front desk. Ryan and Greer exchanged a shrug, amused. In less than a minute she was back, all business as if dressed to direct a board meeting instead of the bathroom. "Follow me, please."

She pressed the elevator button and waved a key card over the sensor to choose the floor. He and Greer dutifully trailed inside and stood back. As they rode up, Ryan noticed she'd pinned a gold name tag to the robe.

Carrie Waller, Deputy Associate Manager

He bit back a smile, the awkward stiffness that overtook him in the hallway easing with amusement at her determined professionalism. Outfit be damned. She was a cute little thing. "I'm Ryan. This is Greer. You must work with Gina."

"Yes." She cleared her throat, repeated the name and title on the tag, and stood a little straighter, lost as she was in the folds of the large robe.

"Will you be at the wedding?" Greer shoved the last of the turkey into his mouth and started opening a ham and cheese. Ryan adjusted the garment bags and held out his hand silently, and Greer grumbled, handing it over.

"I'm coordinating the event." Her phone pinged multiple times and she glanced at it, typing out rapid-fire responses, interspersed by steadying breaths, a combination of stress and competence that stirred Ryan's curiosity.

"Well, you look great." He softened the tease with a smile. "Very winter spa chic. I'm going for the drowned-rat look myself."

Her brows lifted at his joke, lips fighting a smile even as she seemed to shrink slightly in the folds of cloth. "I should have been ready an hour ago, but my sister insisted I wear a different dress, and then my hair was wrong apparently…it's a long story."

"I'll be interested to see the final product. You'll have to save me a dance."

Color flooded her cheeks, gratifying him, and her eyes went wide. Surprised. Interested. A little wary.

She licked her lips and a shot of heat punched his gut, welcome in his still chilled body. "I'll um…see what I can do."

Maybe the whole day wouldn't be all suck. He had to play his role and say goodbye to Ben. But something about Carrie pulled at him, reminded him that this was a party, a celebration. Not just a mission.

The doors glided open, and she marched out, calling *This way, gentlemen* over her shoulder without a backward glance. She led them down the maze of gray hotel hallways, before stopping to knock briskly at room 623, using her key to open the door, and stepping back for them to enter.

"Gunny!" Ben's voice boomed as he came down the short entryway to greet them. "Where the hell have you been? Did you guys come by way of Timbuktu?" He paused, took in their disheveled state. "Or maybe Seattle?"

"Just went for a little run." Ryan tossed his uniform bag over the rail in the open closet and brought Ben in for a hug.

"I'm glad you're here." Ben's voiced dropped in his ear, emotion rasping even as his fist pounded on Ryan's back. "Started thinking I'd have to do this without you."

"We've always got your back, brother." He glanced back to where Carrie's form had been, in the now closed doorway, strangely disappointed she'd disappeared without a word. "Give me five to shower and get dressed."

Ben greeted Greer with similar relief. The three stepped further into the room and a smattering of applause erupted from Ben's other groomsmen and a few fellow Marines from their previous unit. The men lounged around the room with drinks in hand, looking sharp in their suits and dress uniforms, intensifying Ryan's regret at being late. Still, he took a little bow and a massive bite of the sandwich, always the leader. Always in control.

"Do you understand the number of women I've had breathing down my neck over the last twenty-four hours because you dickheads took your sweet time gettin' here, missing the rehearsal and all?" Ben's Oklahoma accent landed heavier on his words, a sure sign of nerves. "Wedding planners, friends, mothers. Not to mention my lovely wife-to-be and all her hotel people."

"Relax, man. All they have to do is stand around and look pretty." Corporal Jake Hodges poured a couple fingers of whiskey and slapped the glass into Ben's grasp with loose grace, suggesting it wasn't his first drink. "Enjoy your last hour of freedom."

Ryan sent Hodges a withering glance and snagged the glass from Ben—who had somehow always been a lightweight, regardless of his muscle and weight—instead pressing a bottle of water into his hands from the ice bucket on the coffee table. "Don't get the groom hammered. It's not a good look."

Ben shrugged, shoulders stiff in the dress blue topcoat, while Hodges took back the glass. "More for me, then." He tossed the amber liquid back in a single long swallow.

"Shit, Hodges, you keep that up and we're going to be shoveling you off the floor before the reception's over." Greer stripped off his wet shirt and pitched it, hitting Hodges in the head as he chased the last drop in the glass.

"Knock it off." Ryan turned on his Gunnery Sergeant voice and stepped between them, giving Hodges a gentle shove onto the couch where Ben's brother Brian watched with amusement. "Shower up, Greer. And be quick, I'm starting to mildew." Then he turned to Ben, looking his friend in the eye. "The wedding will go off without a hitch. I'll make sure of it. You're going to marry that girl and spend the rest of your life making each other happy and nuts and happy all over again. You get me? She won't back out on you because a couple devil dogs showed up late." Ryan smiled, watching his friend nod and settle as he spoke, absorbing the trust and respect reflected in gazes around the room. "She knows what she's getting into."

Here it was. Taking care of his fellow Marines, a purpose that calmed the unmoored sensation in his chest, which had become a constant companion over the last several months. Ryan lifted a bottle of beer from the ice bucket in a toast. "To Gina and Ben and a successful wedding. See you on the other side." The familiar refrain, said to each other before departing for a patrol or simply leaving for company PT. Ben blew out a breath and a smile teased his serious green eyes.

"And wedding fun," Greer called from the bathroom door.

Ryan thought about the intriguing woman in the robe. There was time for fun too. If only for tonight. READ NOW

RESOURCES

This is a work of fiction but deals with sensitive topics, particularly PTSD, and is informed by my personal experience. If you or someone you know is a Veteran struggling with mental health, please reach out for help. You are not alone. Here are a few resources that may be useful.

National Center for PTSD
This department of the VA provides numerous support and crisis services to both Veterans and their families, on the phone and online. Learn more at <u>ptsd.va.gov</u>

Veteran Crisis line
Dial 988 then press 1 or you may text 838255 for a live, online chat.

Veteran Combat Call Center
Call 1-877-WAR-VETS to talk with another combat Veteran or visit <u>vetcenter.va.gov</u> to find community-based counseling for both Veterans and their families.

VA Caregiver Support Line
Call 1-855-260-3274 or visit <u>caregiver.va.gov</u> to find clinical services for caregivers of Veterans.

ACKNOWLEDGMENTS

It's impossible to put into words how much I appreciate my family, my husband, my kids, and my friends for supporting me as I've begun this author journey. Thank you for ignoring the state of our house, yard, and my hair as I put aside cleanliness in the pursuit of words on the page.

Massive thanks in particular to Kristy, Hannah, and Pete for reading early versions of *Wait* and to my editor, Jen Prokop, for helping me find the shape of Gina and Ben's story.

To Sal, for your artistic skills, support, and love. You make me so proud. I hope I can do the same for you.

To all my fellow romance readers and writers out there, I'm so glad to be a part of this community. Thank you for your positivity and welcome.

Finally, to every Veteran, past and present, and the people who love them: Thank you. I hope you see Ben and Gina—and all the other *3000 Reasons* stories—as an accurate representation of the military and veteran experience (albeit, a sexier and more romantic version).

ALSO BY JAIME P. BRADLEY

The 3000 Reasons Series:

Wait: A 3000 Reasons Series Holiday Novella

3000 Reasons to Stay

Reasons to Risk

Reasons to Act

Coming 2026 and 2027

Reasons to Dance

Reasons to Fall

ABOUT THE AUTHOR

Jaime got hooked on romance novels at an inappropriately young age. She's a New England dairy farm kid turned Wyoming cowgirl turned cattle genetics writer, turned romance writer. Jaime lives with her former US Marine husband and spends her days wrangling their four children and numerous farm animals, reading or writing romance novels, binging on romance-related podcasts, and adding more things to her to-do list than she could ever possibly get done.

www.ingramcontent.com/pod-product-compliance
Lightning Source LLC
Chambersburg PA
CBHW062148150726
47991CB00006B/2208